Messandrierre

A Jacques Forêt Mystery

Angela Wren

www.darkstroke.com

Discover us online:
www.darkstroke.com

Join us on facebook:
www.facebook.com/groups/darkstroke

Tweet a photo of yourself holding
this book to **@darkstrokedark**
and something nice will happen.

Dedicated to the lovely couple I met in
the Département of Charente who
invited me for tea and cakes
one afternoon.

An innocent, chance remark whilst chatting
was the single spark that created this story.

Thank you.

Acknowledgments

My most grateful thanks go to all my writing colleagues who have listened patiently, commented constructively and actively encouraged me when my self-belief has deserted me.

I also owe a great debt of gratitude to family and friends who have let me drone on and on about my story without a single groan or complaint.

Lastly, my publishers and editor, and all my fellow authors and readers at Crooked Cat/darkstroke, who are wonderfully supportive.

About the Author

Angela Wren was born and raised in Yorkshire and, having followed a career in Project and Business Change Management, she now works as an Actor and Director at a local theatre.

She has been writing, in a serious way, for about five years. Her work in project management has always involved drafting, so writing, in its various forms, has always been a significant feature throughout Angela's adult life.

She particularly enjoys the challenge of plotting and planning different genres of work. Her short stories vary between contemporary romance, memoir, mystery and historical. She has also written comic flash-fiction and has drafted one-act plays that have been recorded for local radio. The majority of her stories are set in France where she likes to spend as much time as possible each year.

Follow Angela at **www.angelawren.co.uk** and **www.jamesetmoi.blogspot.co.uk**.

The Jaques Forêt Mystery series by Angela Wren:

Messandrierre (#1)
Merle (#2)
Montbel (#3)
Marseille (#4)

Messandrierre

A Jacques Forêt Mystery

it begins

I died beneath a clear autumn sky in September, late in September when warm cévenol afternoons drift into cooler than usual evenings before winter steals down from the summit of Mont Aigoual.

My shallow grave lies in a field behind an old farmhouse. There was no ceremony to mark my death and no mourners, just a stranger in the darkness spading soil over my body. Only the midnight clouds cried for me as they carried their first sprinkling of snow to the tiny village of Messandrierre.

My innocent white coverlet allowing the earth around me to shift and settle unseen and become comfortable again.

september 2007

and then – june 2009

"Jacques, ça va?" A broad smile on his face, Jean-Paul placed the slim bundle of envelopes on the short counter. "How did it go?" He wiped the back of his hand across the beads of sweat just beginning to form on his brow.

"As expected," said Jacques Forêt, his pale blue eyes misted over for a split second as his mind sped back to his parents' home and the sadness of the last few days. He got up from behind his cramped desk and took the single long-legged stride required to reach the public-facing barrier of the village gendarmerie.

"And Paris?" Still a little breathless, Jean-Paul hitched his heavy postbag further up his shoulder and grinned. "How was Paris?"

"Just the same, I think," said Jacques, sifting through the post. "After the funeral I wasn't in the mood to go into the city." He scooped the various items in the delivery together and tapped them level. He needed to keep his thoughts focussed on his work and the new case that had arrived on his desk. "Are you delivering to the mountain farms today?"

"Only the Rouselles and the Pamiers."

"I've only been away for four days, and already a lad has gone missing. He's sixteen, left home in Marseille after an argument with his mother's live-in partner, and was seen in Mende yesterday. But nothing since. There's a photo I've been sent. Taken a couple of months ago." Jacques stepped back to his desk, dropped the post on a desk-pad covered in black and blue doodles and retrieved a batch of stapled pages from one of the red wire trays. He flipped over the first couple of pages and laid the rest flat on the counter.

Jean-Paul pulled the papers towards him and nodded.

"If you see anything unusual—"

"I've still got my delivery in Montbel to do—"

"Just call me," said Jacques, his enunciation a little harsher than intended.

"I can take a detour along the top road if you want?"

"Thanks but it's not necessary." Jacques grinned at the postman's ever-increasing desire to do his job for him. "I'll check the empty properties west of the village first and I've got to go up to Ferme Delacroix anyway, so I'll check out his place, Ferme Sithrez, and the chateau after that. I'll call and question the Pamiers and Rouselles later."

The postman nodded. "Until tomorrow," he said as the glass and metal door rattled shut behind his substantial frame, trapping a blast of warm dusty air inside.

Jacques blew the specks of dust from the papers and, a deep frown forming on his forehead, began to memorise the gaunt, young face. He turned back to the first page. "At home Thursday and Friday morning, last seen Mende around nineteen-thirty…" he read out loud. He paused for a moment and thought about what might have happened. Boys of his age went missing all the time in Paris and Marseille and could remain anonymous, and therefore unrecognised and unfound, for weeks. "I hope it's not a body we find," he said, ripping off one of the sheets with a photo and pinning it on the notice board next to another, faded and yellowed, that had been there for some time. Head down, he took half a step back and ran through the details of the earlier case in his mind.

Kellermann, Dieter Kellermann. German national aged twenty-two. Last seen Mende. Overheard speaking English with a couple, description meagre and thought to be tourists, in May 2008.

He gazed at the older photo. "What the hell happened to you?" His investigator's mind cranked into motion for the first time in twenty-three months, two weeks and two days. It wasn't that he kept tabs on the length of time since he had last been 'effective', as his previous senior officer, a Capitaine in the Judiciaire de Police in Paris, had put it; it was just that he knew. He always knew. He didn't need a note on the calendar, or a red cross to mark the night or the time of the shooting. He instinctively knew. The day. The hour. The moment. And on the anniversary, without thinking or question, he achingly knew.

Darting to the grey filing cabinet in the corner on his left he yanked open the second drawer, pulled out a file and began to leaf through the documents looking for similarities between the two disappearances. There's something, he thought. There might be something. He dumped the file on his desk, slumped down in his chair and ran his hands through his thick dark-brown hair.

"Damn," he muttered under his breath. "Nothing!"

He stared at the papers in front of him, sighed, and then tossed the file in the wire tray. Collecting his blouson jacket, helmet, keys, a second copy of the boy's photo and a dog-eared hand-written note from his desk drawer, he let himself out from behind the counter. He fixed the grubby note to the constantly-there piece of blue-tac on the inside of the door, locked it behind himself and got on his motorbike.

He took the cow track from the village, which ran parallel, for a short distance, to Route Nationale 88, the main interchange between Mende and St Etienne. Taking the first right he called on Gaston, the manager of the local bar, restaurant and campsite. Forty minutes, a fresh warm croissant and coffee later he returned to his bike with no extra or useful information to help locate the missing boy. A right out of the car park in front of the Salle des Fêtes, enabled him to cruise along the D6, where he slowed unnecessarily to take the gently sweeping bend. He'd been doing that a lot, recently, whenever his route or work took him on this particular road out of the village. As he slowly came out of the corner he saw the large entrance porch of the chalet, the garage to the left, the shuttered windows of the snug to the right and the master bedroom to the right of that. Above, the sweeping roof enclosed the glass-fronted loft area. He smiled as he thought back to that Thursday evening the previous year, her warmth and closeness, when they had watched the ever-changing colours in the sky, as a severe thunderstorm had rattled backwards and forwards along the valley.

He parked the bike and toured the exterior of the property. All was as it should be. None of the shutters had been disturbed and everything was locked. Leaving his bike where it was he inspected the remaining four chalets further along the lane and found each of them secure, as he had expected, and with no evidence that the missing boy may have used one of the open patios as a shelter. He rocked the bike off its stand, straddled it and looked at the first chalet again. Not back. And she's not coming back, is she? He revved the Kawasaki's engine into life, let out the clutch and roared up the hill to the fork and took a right along the top road towards the chateau ruins. His cursory search revealed nothing as did his call to the Sithrez who lived in the property just below.

Retracing part of his route, he left the bike on the top road and walked the final sixty metres onto Delacroix's farm and took the opportunity to duck into the open barn before calling at the house. He doubted the boy was there and found no evidence but his pre-existing reason for calling: the farmer's white Lada was parked in its usual place. He circled round, looked at the front windscreen and nodded.

He knocked on the open farmhouse door. As there was no response, he walked straight in and shouted, "Delacroix! Are you there?" The smell of stale food and whisky made his nostrils bristle.

"Gendarme Forêt." Guy Delacroix emerged from the back room. Scruffy in his blue overalls, his thinning grey-black hair a mess, he stood his ground in the doorway between his main room and kitchen. He wiped his blooded hands on an equally blooded rag. "What do you want?" His tone was gruff and uninviting.

Jacques took out his notebook and flicked through to the appropriate page. "On Tuesday last week I pointed out to you that your car tax was out of date. You agreed to get it renewed."

"I did." He sniffed and lifted his chin, a look of defiance in his eyes.

Jacques tensed at the lie. "When? And do you have the receipt for the payment?"

"Of course," said Delacroix as he shuffled across to an old oak dresser that stretched the full distance of the wall at the back of the room. "It's here somewhere," he snapped, sorting through a pile of envelopes and paper. "I'll bring it to the gendarmerie later, when I find it."

"And the disc for display?" The hardness in his own voice made Jacques shift his stance.

"Here! I tell you," he shouted as he thumped his hand on the dresser. "Or maybe on the car, I can't remember what I've done with it."

"Guy, I've already checked the car in the barn," Jacques said, taking a step back. "Unless you have it here and a receipt, I'll put you on a charge right now."

Delacroix rubbed at his hands with the cloth. "All right, all right," he relented. "I haven't got round to it yet." He shrugged.

Jacques waited for an explanation.

Delacroix sighed and seemed to shrink into himself. "Look, Jacques," he said, shuffling forward. "Things are difficult at the moment. It's the money. I just need a couple of weeks and then I will do it."

Casting his policeman's eye around the unkempt room, the pile of newspapers on the windowsill, the numerous used cups, mugs and plates on the stained tablecloth, he sighed. "OK," he said. "But I see you can still afford a good single malt." He stared pointedly at the open, almost empty bottle on the floor between the worn armchair and the ash-covered hearth.

Guy Delacroix shrugged. "It's all I've got."

"End of the month," Jacques said after a moment. "You have until then to get your tax renewed." He pulled out the boy's photo. "One other matter, Guy, have you seen this boy? He might have been in the village yesterday, or if you were in Mende at the weekend you might have seen him there."

Delacroix shook his head. "No. I'm sure I haven't seen him. He looks very young."

"He is," said Jacques as he tucked the photo and his notebook back into his jacket pocket and moved towards the open door. "If you see or hear anything about him let me know, and I will be back on June thirtieth to check on the vehicle. No matter what I am doing that day, I will be back, Guy, and I will expect to see your car properly taxed. Is that understood?"

Delacroix nodded.

As he walked up the steep track to the road, Jacques shook his head. *Sort yourself out, man. Show some self-respect, for God's sake!* The smell of ripe cow dung made him pause and watch the beasts in Delacroix's field behind the barn for a minute or so. Huddled at the gate, their huge hipbones pushing through the soft brown felt of their thin skin, they were lowing constantly and shifting their hooves on the soft muddy ground.

"Fabian, thanks for calling back." Jacques put his foot against the edge of the desk and pushed his chair back the few centimetres available until it scraped against the grey painted wall behind. "I was up at Delacroix's farm before lunch, and I'm not sure if there is a problem, but his cows were all gathered and restless at the gate to the field." He nodded as he listened to the response. "No, no, nothing official." He paused for a moment to make sure he took the right approach. "I'm just concerned, about him, his animals and I'm looking for a favour, that's all… Yes…yes, of course. If you could just call on him and check his livestock I'd appreciate it." Having elicited the response he wanted from the vet in Montbel, he busied himself with paperwork. It wasn't long before his concentration was broken by the usual string of calls: a stolen bicycle, that he knew instantly was really only borrowed, a missing chicken and more in the long-running dispute over the shared boundary between the Delacroix and Rouselle farms.

Later that evening Gaston's wife, Marianne, poured Jacques a glass of beer as he took his usual wooden stool at one end of the bar. "You look tired," she said. "Everything all right?"

He took a long drink of the cool beer and ran his fingers and thumb across his day's growth of dark-brown bristles. "I don't know, Marianne. Today," he said, looking down at his half drunk beer, "today I've achieved nothing!" He smoothed the ripples of condensation on the glass with the back of his forefinger. "A boy is missing and what do I do? I harass an old man about his car tax that he can't really afford. I'm asked to find lost bicycles, and I mediate between feuding farmers." Downing the rest of the beer he dumped the glass back on the bar with a soft thud.

"Ah, Delacroix and the Rouselles." Marianne grinned at him. "But this isn't Paris, Jacques." She refilled his beer and placed it in front of him. "And you knew that when you came here."

"Hmm. But I'm wondering now if I shouldn't go back. At least I would be useful there," he said, the frustration in his voice matching the deep furrow across his forehead.

"But can you just get your old job back in investigation?" Marianne carefully slotted a clean glass back into place on the shelf behind the bar.

"Probably not." He shrugged. "I suppose I'd have to wait for a vacancy and apply." He sipped his beer. "But at least I'd be there to help Thérèse when I wasn't on duty."

Marianne discarded her cloth, folded her arms and leant forward on the bar. "So, that's what this is all about." She took a deep breath. "Jacques, you've just buried your mother and your family is six hundred kilometres away. Of course you will be feeling unsettled. You need time to adjust, that's all."

"Maybe... I don't know." He ran his hands through his hair twice in succession. "I don't know. I'm worried about my sister. She looked all in when I saw her and now she's left with Papa to look after as well as her own family. I feel

I should be doing something useful, you know, rather than —"

The door to the bar swung wide open as two young men barged in.

"Deux cervezas, por favor," shouted the shorter of the two. His dark-blond hair was full of gel and, wearing belted designer jeans with a grey tee shirt, he strutted between the tables towards the bar.

"That's Spanish, you prat!" The taller man, dark haired and wearing a white cotton casual shirt, shoved his hand in the back pocket of his pale-blue jeans and pulled out his wallet. "Excusez mon ami, Madame." His accent was flat and his delivery faltering. "Deux bières, s'il vous plaît," he said and dropped a twenty Euro note on the bar.

Marianne raised her neatly plucked eyebrows at Jacques, pulled the two beers, put them on the counter and left the note where it was. "You pay when you leave," she said in English.

"Right! Thanks." They collected the note and their drinks and moved over to a table.

"When did they arrive?" Jacques was glad of the distraction and instinctively made a mental note of their appearance and clothes. He picked up his own beer and shifted his position slightly so that he could observe them more easily.

"Earlier this afternoon. They're only staying one night."

"Is Gaston here?"

"No, he's in Mende this evening."

"OK. I'll stay until they leave."

Marianne sighed. "Jacques, there's no need. I'll be all right."

"I'll stay just in case."

Smiling her gratitude, she dried the last of the glasses and put it on the shelf. "Beth's back. Did you know?" She turned to face him. "As I was driving past her chalet this afternoon I noticed her car outside."

Blind-sided momentarily by what he'd just heard, Jacques picked up his beer intending to take another drink.

"No." He put the glass back on the bar and began turning it, quarter circle by quarter circle. "No, I didn't know that." He kept his voice flat, unsure of what to say next. "But it doesn't matter." He grabbed that morning's copy of Le Monde from the corner of the bar and scanned the front page without taking in a single piece of information printed there.

Halfway through his third beer, the newspaper finally discarded, he checked his watch. "It's getting late," he said. "And those two are getting raucous. Do you want me to kick them out?"

Marianne glanced at the clock on the wall. "I'll just take them their bill so you can finish that."

She went across to the only occupied table and left a small platter.

"But it's only five past ten," said the shorter one with the blond hair.

"Look, Will, we can probably buy some bottles of wine before we go back to the tents," said his companion. "Come on. I mean, it's not exactly rocking in here, is it?" He stood, collected the glasses, the bill and came to the bar. "Aussi deux," he held up two fingers to demonstrate his meaning. "Deux bouteilles du vin."

Marianne nodded and picked out two bottles of house red, added them to the bill, took the proffered money and gave him his change. "Thank you. Good night," she said in her very precise English.

"We're sorted, Will. Come on, let's go."

They left with Forêt following a discreet distance behind. Standing in the lee of the building he watched them disappear across the children's playground, up the log steps on the bank leading to the camping area and into the trees, their loud voices reverberating across the dark and silent valley.

Jacques turned and walked the length of the exterior of the bar to the car park fully intending to cross it, but Marianne's words kept circling in his mind. Without understanding why, he turned right out of the car park and followed the D6 around the sweeping bend towards Beth's chalet. When he looked up he saw that the shutters on the master bedroom were pinned back, framing a low yellow light from the windows. He quickened his pace.

What am I doing? He stopped, let out a deep sigh, zipped up his leather jacket, turned and walked back home.

tuesday

Beth Samuels stretched and yawned as she waited for her coffee to be ready. Two consecutive days behind the wheel of her black Audi had taken their toll. She gathered her midnight-blue silk dressing gown closer around her and pulled the belt tight, as the coffee gurgled its readiness to be poured. Cupping her mug in both hands, she walked through the kitchen and across the main room to the front door. She pulled back the bolts, unlocked and opened it fully. Releasing the catches on the exterior wooden door, she went outside onto the entrance porch, took a deep breath, and listened to the silence of the morning. A smile crept across her pale face as she gazed at the uninterrupted expanse of fields and trees to the mountain peaks beyond.

She stepped off the porch, sauntered down the short path and watched as the strengthening sun lifted the overnight dew from the lush grass of the hillside opposite. In the distance, she could just hear the flat clank of cowbells as Fermier Rouselle and his herd of Aubracs reached the last few metres of the steep path to the high pastures.

"Bonjour," said a voice from a little way behind her.

Momentarily startled she turned. "Jacques!" Smiling fleetingly, she took a step back.

"A little early for you, I think," he said, grinning at her.

"Perhaps." She raised her mug to her lips and took a sip.

"It's really good to see you again."

Beth wouldn't let herself respond immediately, she was afraid she might say too much.

"Are you staying long?" He stepped closer and placed his hands on the top rung of the five-bar gate.

Relaxing a little, she turned to him and gave him a half

15

smile. "Just until the end of the month, Jacques, that's all." She looked away again as she focused her attention on her coffee.

"And…how are things at home?"

She turned her face up towards the sun and tossing her long black hair behind her shoulders she took a deep breath. "Umm…difficult. It's been a very difficult year, as I'm sure you realise," she said and looked straight at him, her hazel eyes filled with sadness. "But I'm beginning to…" She watched the steam gently rising from her coffee and let her voice and the unfinished sentence drift away.

He shrugged. "OK. If…well, if I can help with anything…" he said, rubbing his hand along the top of the gate. "I'd better be going and you know where I am if you need me."

She nodded but did not reciprocate his smile. To prevent herself from calling after him, she turned and hurried back along the path. On the bottom step leading up to the porch, she stopped and stared at the square black planter to her left as if seeing it for the first time. Slowly mounting the last two steps, she bent down and pulled the pot forward and the few remaining brown leaves on the almost bare bush of branches drifted to the ground.

"So, the winter got to you too," she said, picking up the brittle debris and tossing it on top of the soil. She pushed the wooden exterior door completely back and secured it in place and then repositioned the planter in front of it. With some reluctance, she went back inside, but left the front door open.

The place seemed airless and musty. She moved past the foot of the spiral stairs and opened the door on her right into the snug. The white of her trainers on the black granite hearth in front of the fireplace, exactly where she had left them to dry out all those months ago, captured her attention from the gloominess inside the room. She blinked back the first prickles of tears and sighed as she consciously reminded herself of her reason for returning to the chalet.

Rob Myers had a blinding headache when he finally woke up at a little after eleven. His fellow student and travelling companion, Will Coulson, had been up for a good two hours when Rob crawled out of his tent, eyes bleary, hair a mess and reeking of last night's alcohol.

"Shit, I feel crap," he said running his hand across his pale and black bristled face.

"Yeah, so did I at first. The showers are really hot here. You'll be OK after that. And I've been to the baker's already, and we've still got some bacon, so I'll do us some butties." Will waited for his mate to respond or move. "Rob, shift yourself, will you!"

"Yeah, yeah," said Rob, as another wave of nausea passed over him. He grabbed the saddle of his nearby bicycle and steadied himself and then disappeared back into his tent and re-emerged with a towel and wash-bag. "I'll be back in ten."

Will thought only once about getting the tiny stove set up and dismissed it immediately as a more interesting occupation had a greater draw on his attention. Moving round to his own tent, he resumed his vantage point with Rob's camera and telephoto lens in readiness and waited. He'd already got some good shots, but there was always the possibility of more.

***

The warmth of the afternoon and the tedium of cleaning alone in the chalet had driven Beth outside. Her tripod and camera already set up on the porch, she made the fine adjustments to get the picture she wanted. The sun wasn't quite at the right angle to give the depth of shadow in the valley she required, but she could wait. She got herself a cold beer and a book from the shelves in the snug and settled down on the bench in the shade.

"Bonjour," shouted Rob from the road. "Belle vue!" He

held up his camera, and pointed.

Unsure to whom the greeting was directed, Beth looked around and took a moment before responding. "Oui," she said and then considered the two passers-by more carefully. The pallor of their skin, the shorter man's hair colouring and their clothes made her smile in recognition. "I'm English, too," she said as she got up and walked over to the low, white-painted, wooden fence. "On holiday?"

"Yeah, sort of," said Rob. "We're taking a couple of weeks to cycle down to Argelès on the south coast where we've both got summer jobs in a beach bar."

"Yeah, we're just passing through, really," added Will.

"That's quite a journey. It took me two days to drive from Calais to here." She took a drink of her beer. Indicating her glass, she said, "Can I offer you one?"

"Thanks a lot," said Rob.

"Gate's over there," she said. "Come in and make yourselves comfortable on the bench there and I'll get the beers."

"I'm Beth," she said when she returned with a tray and put it down on the floor. "And help yourselves." Going back inside, she got a folding chair from the boot room behind the kitchen and joined her guests on the porch.

***

Jacques strolled through the village to a small house with a very neat, well-planted front garden. Madame Mancelle answered his knock on the open door.

"Marie, I'm hoping Pierre is back from school. There's something I'd like to discuss with him."

A worried look crossed her face. "Is he in trouble, Jacques?"

"No, no, there's no need to concern yourself. He's… helping me with my enquiries."

Relief gave way to a broad smile as she bustled inside and delivered her son to her visitor.

"Shall we take a stroll, Junior Gendarme Mancelle?"

Towering over his five-year-old assistant, Jacques strode further down the street, then stopped and sat on the low wall surrounding the churchyard. "Now, Pierre, I thought we had an agreement." He looked at the wide-eyed, small, round face that stared up at him, and in the absence of a response, Jacques continued, keeping his voice low and calm. "I thought we agreed that you would stop borrowing the bike belonging to Jean Pamier without his permission if I promised not to tell your parents." Again there was absolute silence from his young charge. "Well?"

Pierre sat up, his spine ramrod straight. "Yes, Gendarme Forêt," he blurted out.

Jacques frowned. "So, that means that I have a theft but no criminal to pin it on." He shook his head in mock and mild confusion before continuing. "You see, Monsieur Pamier tells me that the bike is missing again and if you have kept your side of the bargain then I really don't know how I can solve this terrible crime." He folded his arms across his chest and waited.

"Maybe it was Alain. Yes! It must have been Alain." Nodding vigorously, the boy looked at Jacques. "I'm sure it was him on the bike on Sunday."

"Is that so? Hmm. But Monsieur Pamier said the bike only went missing yesterday lunch-time." He looked down and saw that Pierre was paying great attention to his grubby fingernails. "So, Pierre, what to do? What to do!" Finally, taking out his notebook he pretended to write. "Tuesday, Pierre Mancelle charged with theft of a bike…"

"Please, Gendarme Forêt." His eyes filled with tears. "Please don't arrest me. I won't do it again, I promise. I really, really promise this time."

"OK," he said handing the boy his handkerchief. "I won't arrest you if you tell your parents yourself what you have been up to."

The boy's eyes widened as another stream of tears dribbled down his cheeks. "But…but Maman will kill me."

Jacques suppressed a smirk with some difficulty. "Well, I don't think she will, she's your mum. But she might give you some chores to do for a week or so or stop your pocket money perhaps. So, what's it to be? Admit or arrest?"

Head down, Pierre whimpered a couple of times and then reluctantly nodded his agreement to confess his misdemeanour to his parents.

"All right, Junior Gendarme Mancelle. Stand up straight. Wipe your face. And march!"

Jacques escorted the boy back to his house to find his mother waiting, not anxious but curious, at the front gate. "Marie, your son has been very helpful and I believe he has something to tell you."

Jacques nodded to Pierre as a prompt and the whole story came tumbling out in a mass and confusion of words.

Leaving the mother to deal with her child, he strolled back to his office, a wide grin on his face. As the final task of the day he stood in front of the photo of the missing boy from Marseille and began to remove the drawing pins from the notice board. Scruffy, hungry, but unharmed, the youngster had turned up at his uncle's house in St Chely late the previous night.

wednesday, january 27th, 1954

The glistening white snow crunched under her small black Wellingtons as she ran back to the cottage. Her breath was fast and misted the instant it hit the cold mountain air. Her cherry red cheeks were streaked with dried tears.

"Mama!" She paused and looked down the snowy track behind her. All she could see was a trail of footprints. Running on, she wailed out the word again, "Mama!"

She missed her footing on a slippery tree-root and hit the snow hard. Winded, she lay there for a moment and let the icy wetness seep into her duffle coat. Fractious and whimpering she pulled herself to her feet, but the doll. Where was the doll? The doll that she had asked for. The doll that was supposed to be hers. The doll that had been given to her sister instead. She looked around and spotted the toy's Christmas coloured coat with the black velvet collar just ahead of her, also face down in the snow. A small glaring red figure and a sanguine prompt that she needed to hurry. A sly smile crossed her face as she retrieved the toy and hugged it. She raced on. "Mama!" The bothy was just beyond the large oak tree where she and her younger sister had played for the first time in the summer.

This time her mother appeared at the door in answer and came towards her. "Ana, what is it?" She squatted down as her child rushed into her arms and mewled in a fresh convulsion of tears.

"And Gosia?" The mother looked over her daughter's shoulder and along the path to the frozen loch, the disturbed snow her only evidence for her growing fears. "Gosia... Oh God!" Clutching her daughter to her, she stood frozen to the spot. "Oh my God!"

She screamed out her youngest child's name again and ran...and ran.

saturday, june, the present

It was clear that Will Coulson was worried when he walked through the open door of the gendarmerie. His face had lost its brightness, there were dark shadows under his grey eyes, and his initial report to Jacques was earnest and angst-ridden. Jacques came back into the cubby-hole that served as an interview room and put a mug of coffee on the tiny table in front of Will.

Picking up the statement, he resumed the interview in English. "So, Rob Myers, your travelling companion, aged twenty-two, was last seen by you at the campsite here in Messandrierre around two on Wednesday afternoon." Jacques looked at Will for confirmation and he nodded in response. "And on that day, before you separated, you both agreed to meet at the campsite in Mende on Thursday. That was the day before yesterday."

"Yeah. We were going to try out this night club on Friday." Will nursed his coffee.

"The place on Causse d'Auge?"

"Umm..." From his wallet he pulled out a card and studied it. "Yeah," he said, putting it on the table facing Jacques. "A mate of mine found it last year when he was here and said it was full of...well. He said it was a good place."

Jacques stared at him. Full of women is what you really meant to say. "OK. And when Rob didn't arrive in Mende on Thursday, you did what?"

"Well, nothing to start with. I just thought he was onto a good thing, that's all."

"A good thing?"

"This woman we'd met on Tuesday. Rob's really into

photography and so was she. They were getting on well, if you know what I mean." He shuffled in his chair and picked up his coffee.

Jacques sat back and waited to see if he would say more, but was disappointed. "And on Friday, when he still didn't turn up?"

"I just texted him. 'S'pose she's worth it.' That's all I put."

"What time was that?"

He shrugged. "Don't know. About eleven-ish, lunchtime or something like that." He picked up the mug, took another sip and put it to one side and leaned forward on the table. "Then when he didn't turn up in time to go the club I phoned him but his phone was switched off."

"How can you be sure of that? Perhaps the battery was flat."

"No, he's got his charger with him. He never lets it get flat."

Jacques grinned. "Perhaps he didn't want to be interrupted. He's twenty-two, got a woman…"

Will sat up. "No. You don't understand. He doesn't turn his phone off. He uses it constantly and he always responds to texts. And when he misses a call he always calls back or texts. He just doesn't turn it off like that." He stared at Jacques. "He doesn't. He just doesn't!" He thumped the table with the flat of his hand in frustration. "And all his gear is missing too. I've been back to the campsite. His stuff's all gone. His bike, his tent, everything."

"OK. Calm down."

"Well, do something then," shouted Will. "He's gone. He wouldn't just bunk off like that. He's a good mate."

Jacques picked up the statement again and in a low voice said, "I will look into it but let's get all the details first. And you need to understand that Rob, in the eyes of the law, is a responsible adult and he is free to move around as he chooses." However, in Jacques' mind, there were strong possible similarities with a previous case. "This woman he was with. Do you have any details? A name, an address?"

Will frowned for a moment. "She's here. Right now!"

"I need you to be as precise as possible, Will. The more detail I have the better the chance…"

"The chalet!" He stared at Jacques. "Over there!" He jabbed out his right arm and quickly withdrew it as the pain of hitting the wall reverberated through his hand and wrist. "Shit!"

Jacques maintained an expressionless face despite the provocation. He kept hold of the statement and his pen, but the sinking feeling in his stomach, as he realised that Beth was most likely the woman in question, was undeniable. He swallowed hard. "I need a name, Will," he said. His tone steady and unemotional.

"Beth. She said her name was Beth." Will rubbed his hand and then stretched out his fingers.

"And a description," said Jacques even though he could have written it himself without prompting. He put the statement on the table and began writing again as Will talked.

"She's got long black hair. Umm…she was about five foot five, may be five-six tall, I guess. Slim and she was in the chalet on the far side of the camping. The first one on the left as you go up the hill."

"And you saw her last on Tuesday?"

Will slumped back in his chair. "Tut…yeah!" He watched as the biro traced the words on the page.

With the final full stop in place, Jacques carefully collected together the various pages and put them in order.

Will sat up and challenged his interviewer. "Well? Are you going to arrest her, then?"

"It's not that simple, Will." Jacques turned the papers round, placed them on the table and handed over his pen. "Sign here, here and here, please," he said. "Lastly, write your contact details for here in France and in England on this sheet, please."

Back at his own desk, Jacques went through the statement again and mentally notched up the number of similarities with the Kellermann case. A count of four was low but, at this stage of an investigation, could neither be ignored nor relied upon. With his scruffy hand-written note back in place on the door he locked up and walked across to the bar.

"Jacques." Gaston checked the clock on the wall. "You're a bit early for lunch if you're eating here today."

"No, Gaston. This is official."

Gaston's welcoming smile disappeared as he came out from behind the bar. "We'd better sit then," he said and moved to a table set for two in the corner.

"Two Englishmen camped here on Monday and I just need a few details from you."

"I'll just get the book," he said. He returned with two record-cards and a large receipt book and sat opposite Jacques. "William Coulson and Robert Myers," he said. "Both had tents and were cycling through to the south coast, I think." He handed over the registration cards. "These are the details they gave me when they arrived."

Jacques looked at Myers' card first and jotted down the passport number in his notebook. Everything else, Myers' full name, home address, nationality and date of arrival he already knew. Although he had Coulson's details he still examined the card to make sure the information was consistent. "And they both arrived together on Monday?"

Gaston nodded.

"Can you remember what time?"

"Of course. Marianne had just left to collect Stephanie from the lycée in Mende, so it would have been sixteen-fifteen, sixteen-twenty, but no later."

Jacques made a note. "And how did they seem to you?"

Gaston shrugged. "The same as always," he said. "Foreign tourists. Loud. Bad French. And they were talking all the time."

"Did you pick up anything from their conversation?"

"Not really," he said. "You know how it is. They just wanted to get through the paperwork and I wanted to make sure they paid."

Jacques nodded. "And how did they pay?"

"In cash, but only for that one night." Gaston opened the receipt book, placed it on the table and pointed to an entry half way down the page. "There," he said. "They shared the one emplacement and they each paid half the cost. This entry here was for the next day when they came in to pay for a second night."

Jacques made another note. "So that was Tuesday?"

Gaston nodded again. "Marianne dealt with that. And it was also cash."

"Do you know what time on Tuesday they came in and paid for that night?"

Gaston thought for a moment or two as he smoothed down his drooping moustache with his thumb and forefinger. "It was whilst I was out and I got back here about twelve-thirty, had lunch... Yes, Marianne mentioned it then."

"So, they decided to stay longer some time that morning," said Jacques, more to himself than to his interviewee. "Mm...why would they do that?" He looked at Gaston. "And what about Wednesday when Coulson left? Did you see either of them that day?"

"First thing that morning I did my usual tour of the site and their two tents were still there. A biker was on emplacement twenty-two at the top and he was packing up to leave." Glancing down at his receipt book, he tapped the next entry with his forefinger. "He must have arrived late the previous night so, I just took his name, Camping Card number and bike registration," he said and pointed to the scribbled note on the page opposite. "And collected the cash from him."

Jacques examined the handwritten details. "So he was French," he said as he made his own notes. "Did you or Marianne see Coulson leave?"

"I don't know about Marianne, but I didn't see Coulson leave. When I did my evening tour there was only one tent on that spot and no-one else on the site."

"And what about Myers? Did you see him on Wednesday

at all?"

"Only when he came to pay for that night's camping." Gaston turned over the page and pointed to the first entry. "It was just before lunch and he paid in cash."

"And how did he seem to you?"

Gaston smiled. "Quieter than his friend, and more polite."

"Did he say anything about why he was staying on by himself?"

"No." Gaston thought for a moment. "Can I ask what this is all about?"

Jacques sighed. "It's just a routine enquiry about a tourist who hasn't turned up as expected."

Gaston looked him in the eye. "But you think it's more serious?"

"I'm just making preliminary enquiries, Gaston, that's all." He disliked having to take 'the official line' with his neighbours and friends, but it was all part of the job. His job. Fleetingly, he wished he was back in Paris and surrounded by the anonymity of that vast city. "What about Thursday?"

"The same. His tent was there first thing and gone when I went round in the evening."

"Do you know if Marianne saw him leave?"

Gaston frowned. "No. Well, I don't think so and if she did she didn't mention it."

"Is Marianne around for me to talk to?"

"She's in the kitchen getting ready for lunch." Gaston checked his watch. "We have three tables booked for twelve-fifteen, so can that wait?"

Jacques made a final note. "Of course. Thanks, Gaston, and I'll be in tonight for a couple of beers. I'll talk to Marianne then."

Out in the sunshine, Jacques climbed the log steps and went straight to emplacement seven and looked over the ground. Apart from a stray sweet wrapper and a small but deep indentation in the soil where a stone had been there was nothing to suggest or indicate that anything sinister had occurred. An examination of the nearby hedgerow revealed the offending rock. He rolled it backwards and forwards with the tip of his pen, it had clearly just been tossed aside to make the pitch smoother. Standing in the middle of the camping spot Jacques slowly turned round and took in the view from all sides. In his notebook he drew a rough sketch and then, at the bottom corner, noted the compass points. Looking to his right again he saw Beth's chalet through the trees. He hesitated, but then walked back to his office.

***

Beth checked that her camera and tripod were steady on the impromptu plinth that she had erected that morning at the side of the garage. She finalised the focus, re-checked the shot and, satisfied she would get the series of pictures she wanted, set the time-lapse function. Walking round to the front of the chalet she collected her rucksack, moved her bike out on to the road and freewheeled down the slope to the N88. She peddled furiously up the steep incline of the main road and was a little out of breath when she reached the brow, but soon recovered as she coasted down the other side and turned right onto the narrow lane to Montbel. It was just two when she leant her bike against the metal parking bar in front of the small supermarket.

"The French will take offence at you locking up your bike, you know," said a soft but mature English voice at the side of her. She looked up as she clicked the lock into place.

"It's not the done thing round here," continued the tall elderly man with grey hair as he took another step towards her.

A kind face, she thought as she responded to his smile. "It's not the French I'm worried about," she said grinning. "It's all those noisy English tourists!"

"Luckily, I can't ride a bike anymore. Arthritic knee, you know." He extended his right hand for her to shake. "I'm John, by the way."

"Beth," she said.

"Are you here for the summer?"

"No, no." She wondered just how much to say to this stranger. His hound's tooth jacket was very traditional and had probably been expensive when it was new. She glanced at his leather shoes and decided they would have been equally costly. "I'm just passing through, really," she said. "Just here for a couple of weeks or so. And you?"

"Oh, we live here now. My wife, Clair, and I have a small farmhouse in the next village. She wants to make some scones this afternoon but we've run out of raisins…" Interrupted by the metal shutter on the shop entrance being wound up he paused and checked the time. "A typical French two o'clock," he said as he showed Beth his wristwatch, which recorded the time as eight minutes past the hour.

"Well, must get the shopping done," she said striding ahead to collect her basket. "Nice to meet you." She smiled and went straight to the fresh fruit and vegetables before he had chance to resume the conversation. Keeping her head down she moved swiftly from aisle to aisle and managed to avoid any further contact with the man. However, whilst waiting at the only open checkout she began to feel guilty about her lack of cordiality and wished that she hadn't been quite so dismissive. But she didn't want to explain. It was too difficult to explain. As she packed her purchases into her rucksack she noticed John waiting in the queue to pay. A broad smile crossed her face. "I hope you enjoy the scones," she said, and waved and left.

***

With the information gathered from Gaston and Will typed up and filed, Jacques had no more excuses for putting off his visit to Beth. Since seeing her again on Tuesday, he had not been able to stop thinking about her. In truth, she had been on his mind for the last twelve months. But, he hadn't seen her all week, and now his only excuse to call was on police business. Walking across to her chalet, he kept re-assuring himself that there would be a sound reason for Myers' apparent disappearance and that Beth's involvement could only be cursory. His pace slowed as he rounded the bend approaching her place.

"Facts," he said to himself as his shoes scrunched on the gravel of her short driveway. "Facts and direct evidence." He removed his cap and ran his hands through his hair, and then knocked.

When he got no response after knocking again he decided to go back to the bar to interview Marianne instead. Half way down the path he looked up and saw Beth steadily cycling round the sweeping bend to her chalet. He smiled as he watched her. But his visit was official and, taking a deep breath, he walked to the front gate, opened it and waited. Beth stopped just short of the turn into her drive and after a moment began to wheel her bike up towards him.

"Bonjour, Jacques."

Her voice seemed expressionless and constrained to him but he smiled. "Beth, I was hoping to have a word with you if you have the time," he said, closing the gate behind her.

"What about?" She looked at him directly, her voice flat and her brow furrowed.

"I'm making some enquiries about a tourist who was here a couple of days ago." He took a step back and indicated the chalet with his left hand. "Perhaps we can talk inside?"

With only the glimmer of a smile on her face, Beth moved past him. "Yes, of course." She leaned her bike against the garage door and then led him into the kitchen. "I'll make us some coffee." She put her rucksack full of shopping on the floor. "Or would you prefer a beer?"

"Coffee's fine," he said and took out his notebook. "On Monday two campers, Robert Myers and William – or Will – Coulson were in the village. Did you see them or meet them?"

"Yes, I did. When was it? Umm…the day after I got here. Tuesday. Mm. Tuesday afternoon." She put the coffee pot on the hob and crossed to the fridge, then stopped. "Sorry, I

31

forgot. You have your coffee black, don't you? And please sit down, Jacques. I know this is business, but having you standing there, in uniform like that, is making me nervous."

He heard the slight tremor in her voice and pulled a stool towards himself. "So, Tuesday," he said in a softer tone as he sat down.

She positioned her own stool at the furthest corner of the breakfast bar and sat. "Umm…yes…they came down the hill whilst I was outside with my camera. I wanted some shots of the valley and the hills opposite. The sun wasn't right, so I got myself a beer and a book and read whilst I waited, and they spoke to me."

"Can you remember which of them spoke to you first?"

"Rob. He also had a camera and said he was very keen on photography."

"And Will was with him?" She nodded. "What time was this?"

She thought for a moment and when the coffee pot glugged, she got up and turned off the hob. "I'm not sure. Must have been around three, maybe three-thirty in the afternoon." She put Jacques' coffee on the bar in front of him and returned to her stool with her own.

"Thanks. And what happened then?"

"I got some beer for them and we chatted. Mostly about photography. And then they went." She sipped her coffee as he made his notes.

"And what time did they leave?"

"About six, I think, or just after. Hmm, yes about eighteen-ten."

"Did they say anything about where they were going?" Jacques noticed that her frown had returned and that she was twisting her wedding ring round and round her finger. He wondered why. "Or, perhaps, they mentioned what their plans were?" Putting his notebook down, he observed her as she formed her response. A moment later, when he recognised that she was avoiding his gaze, he prompted her gently. "Anything they said could be helpful, Beth."

"But that's the point. Had I known you would be here

today asking me about them I would have paid more attention. But it was just chitchat, you know. They said something about working for the summer." She looked at the floor. "I know they're travelling south but I can't remember the name of the place they're heading to. It was certainly a name I didn't recognise."

Jacques already knew where and which bar but he kept the details supplied by Coulson to himself. He was more interested in what they had told her and, if there was a difference, how different that story might be.

"I know Rob's from Leeds," she said. "So we talked about places at home that we both knew. And I picked up a few really good tips from him about photography but I can't see how that would help you..." She stopped and looked at Jacques directly. "I've just realised something. I don't know what information would help you because you haven't actually said what this is all about, have you?"

And there it was again. The sinking feeling in the pit of his stomach. "It's just routine, Beth," he said calmly. "There's nothing for you to worry about." As he turned the page in his notebook, he looked her in the eye and asked his next question. "How did Rob and Will seem to you? By that I mean how did they come across to you as people?"

She smiled and seemed to relax a little. "Oh, that's much easier," she said. "Rob was very polite and his conversation was intelligent." Another frown crossed her face as she thought for a moment. "Will didn't really say that much, but when he did he mostly made jokes at Rob's expense and I got the impression that Rob was the more sensible of the two."

"They were camped just the other side of the road, and from their emplacement there's a reasonably clear view across to this chalet. Did you notice them on the campsite at any time whilst they were here?"

"No. Not really. It never occurred to me to look." She stared into her empty mug and sighed, then she stood and brought the coffee pot over. "Would you like some more?"

"No, thanks. So you didn't see them leave?"

Reaching into a drawer she pulled out a mat and placed it under the coffee pot. "No. I just happened to be out on the porch when they walked past on Tuesday afternoon. If it hadn't been so warm I wouldn't even have... Sorry. I'm blabbering on about stuff that is of no use to you, aren't I?"

"No. It doesn't matter." He smiled and put his notebook away. "OK. That's all I think. Thanks for the coffee. I'll let myself out."

***

Beth watched him as he strode through the main room to the front door. She thought about going after him but her feet wouldn't respond. The click of the front door, as he opened it forced her to a decision.

"Jacques...before you go..." But the door had closed behind him and the moment was gone. "The guns... If you meant what you said the other day, I really need some help with the guns." She sighed, picked up her rucksack and began to empty out her shopping into the fridge. Closing the door, she leant back against it. "This is intolerable," she said to the empty room as she slid down and sat on the cool tiled floor. "You just need to come right out and tell him, Beth."

She propped her elbows on her knees and rubbed her fingers in circles on either side of her forehead as if doing so would modify or eradicate her memory of their time together the previous year. But it remained. Unaltered.

***

Jacques smiled as he strolled down the hill and notched up Beth remembering how he had his coffee as a good sign. The church clock chimed four, twice in succession, as he walked across the car park to the bar to interview Marianne. Once that last piece of work was complete, the evening would then be his own and he considered how he might spend the time. He realised that the possibility of a second call at Beth's chalet, out of uniform, was growing more attractive by the second.

Marianne was busy at work on the books at a table by the window when he walked through the open door. "Ah, Jacques. Gaston said you would be back to talk to me."

"I just want to know what you can tell me about Myers and Coulson," he said, sitting down opposite her.

"Nothing, really. They arrived on Monday and paid for a second night's camping on Tuesday. The blond one left on Wednesday and the other one on Thursday. That's it," she said.

Jacques referred to his notebook. "Gaston said he thought you might have seen Coulson leave on Wednesday."

Marianne thought for a moment and then turned back the pages of the large diary in front of her and pointed at a name scrawled across the sheet. She nodded. Next, she chose and counted a small number of receipts from the carefully laid out piles of paper for each day of the week. "Wednesday, we had only the one booking for lunch that day but another four tables were taken. So I finished a bit earlier than usual and no, I didn't see Coulson leave, but I did notice that he had gone when I walked up to the mobile home in emplacement thirty-two. I'd washed the curtains last weekend and I went to put them back up ready for the booking for this coming week."

"And what about Myers, did you see him at all on Wednesday or Thursday?"

"Oh yes. On both days he was at…" And then she paused, and turned her face away as if reluctant to say anymore.

Jacques looked up from his notebook. "Marianne?"

"He was at Beth's on Wednesday afternoon."

"OK," he said. He could feel the pit of his stomach tightening once again. "What exactly did you see?"

She stared out of the window for a moment. "As I walked back from the mobile home I saw the two of them on the porch."

"And you are sure that was Wednesday afternoon and not Tuesday?"

"Yes."

"And it was just Beth and Rob Myers."

She nodded.

"What time was this?"

"I'm not sure. Late afternoon, I suppose."

"What about Thursday?"

"The baker in Montbel doesn't deliver on Thursdays and Sundays so I or Gaston have to go over to Rieutort du Randon on the other side of the col. I was driving past Beth's chalet at about eleven on my way to fetch the bread, and I saw Rob Myers on her driveway about to go to her front door. He had his bike and all his gear with him."

Jacques could feel the colour beginning to drain from his face. "And when you drove by on your way back, what did you see?"

"Nothing."

"And you didn't pass him on your route to and from Rieutort."

"No."

The gendarmerie was silent apart from the sound of Jacques' boots as he paced backwards and forwards on the hard wooden floor behind the counter. It took him about fifteen minutes to order his thoughts and a single moment to change his mind about how he would spend his evening. He stopped and looked at Kellermann's photo on the wall. No, it's not possible. Going to his desk he picked out the relevant papers from the wire tray and went through them. Beth was here last May also. He sighed and pulled out the page with Rob's photo on it and started to pin it to the notice board. "So, Monsieur Myers, from Beth's chalet you could go up the road to Rieutort or down the road to Mende." The first drawing pin was pressed firmly into place. "We know you apparently didn't get to Mende, so, did you go up the road?" The second and third pins were driven home. "But as Marianne didn't pass you on the Rieutort road, did you take the right fork towards the chateau?" With the photo securely in place he took a short step back and folded his arms. "Or is it that you never left…"

The shrill bleating of the phone on the desk demanded his attention.

"Gendarmerie Messandrierre." He listened as Fermier Rouselle explained the situation. "…OK, and has the vet been informed?… But the animal is still alive?… Are you sure we can handle this ourselves without the Fire Brigade?… Yes, all right. I'll be there."

He replaced the handset, grabbed his overalls and hurriedly pulled them on over his uniform. He wondered about his gun secured in the bottom drawer of the desk. No. The vet can do that if required. His hand-written note in place, he locked the door and sprinted through the cattle tunnel under the N88 and headed up the track to the high pasture where one of Rouselle's cows was stranded in a ditch with a possible broken leg.

monday

"...the missing tourist investigation is ongoing. I still have one possible witness to interview and that will be done today. But so far there is nothing to indicate foul play," said Jacques as he made his regular report to his senior officer, Gilles Fournier, in Mende.

"Leave it, then. He's an adult who hasn't turned up as expected. Leave it," said Fournier. "I'm assigning Thibault Clergue to you from tomorrow for the rest of the week. We've had three reports of poaching in the woods surrounding Messandrierre." He held out a file of papers for Jacques to take. "Details in here. I want the two of you to find the culprit. The summer season is almost with us and we need this individual and his or her companions stopped before all the tourists arrive. On Saturday next we also have a demonstration against the transportation of nuclear waste here in Mende, and I will need both you and Clergue to report here at seven that morning. Understood?"

Jacques nodded and left. There was never any point in questioning or disagreeing with Fournier because he always pulled rank. And when that didn't work he automatically resorted to shouting and verbal intimidation. Fournier for a colleague, as Jacques had realised within a few weeks of taking up his post in Messandrierre, was like working for a robot. He never smiled or joked with his men. He never lunched or went out for a beer with them and, if rumour was to be believed, he even refused invitations from his senior colleagues.

"That man's a machine," said Jacques as he closed the office door and made his way out to the yard where his bike was parked. The engine started, he let out the clutch. He had just enough time to get to the village restaurant for lunch.

***

"Now, my little one. Where have you been? I've been looking for you all day," Clair said, scooping up the creature from the tiled floor. "And you weren't there, sweetie. You weren't anywhere." She ran her hand over the silky tabby-coloured fur and provoked a long low purr in response. Another long, slow stroke and then her hand moved to the cat's ear and she gently squashed it between her fingers again and again. Her wide blue eyes narrowed as she stared at the cat.

"Where have you been?" She pronounced the words slowly and deliberately and then let the animal drop to the floor.

"I met that nice young lady at the supermarket again," said John, as he reached over and unlatched the bottom half of the stable door leading into the old farmhouse kitchen. "Remember I told you about her the other day." He placed two heavy bags of shopping on the pink and white floral oilcloth covering the dining table.

Clair lit a cigarette. "Yes, I remember," she said and waited whilst John removed all of the shopping and placed it on the table in rows carefully organised by product type. Delving into the bottom of one of the bags he found the till receipt and smoothed it out before he handed it to his wife.

"I think I've got everything," he said.

"And the list?" She held out her hand.

"Oh yes. In my pocket," he said, producing a crumpled white envelope with a corner missing where the stamp had once been.

Clair began checking the list and as she found each item she handed it to John to put away. "I can't remember what you said her name was," she said with the cigarette hanging from the corner of her mouth. Her attention turned to the list again, and she handed him a large bunch of broccoli and some celery.

"Beth," he said, returning from the walk-in pantry.

She then checked the dairy produce. "I thought you said she was only here for a day or so."

John frowned. "Erm…she said she was…erm…passing through. Yes, that was it. But today she said she was here in Messandrierre and would be here for at least another couple of weeks."

Clair grinned and moved onto the line of tinned vegetables and soups. "Well, we'd better do the neighbourly thing then, darling, and invite her over. Shall I make scones and cake for tea on Thursday?"

"What was that?" A muffled noise emerged from behind the open fridge door.

"Scones," said Clair, her deep gravel voice louder but encouraging, "for tea on Thursday. What do you think?"

John lumbered back into the kitchen and pulled the pantry door shut. "Why not? And shall we invite Beth?" For a moment his smile widened at the thought and then just as quickly disappeared behind a puzzled frown. "But I don't know where she's staying," he said, his visible disappointment almost child-like.

Clair took a long drag on her cigarette and tapped the ash into a little porcelain dish on the sideboard. "Don't worry, darling, it's a very small village. I'll find her for you."

***

In the snug Beth was going through cupboards and shelves. On the floor beside her were various piles of books on cars, motorbikes, fishing and hunting along with a selection of well-worn paperbacks, mostly adult adventure with some horror and sci-fi, all of which had been Dan's. Moving them out of her way, she got up and brought a large cardboard box from the boot room and began to stack them inside, then dragged the heavy box out and left it by the door. She heard the front gate squeak as Jacques opened and closed it.

"Now what?" She sighed and pulled the duster out of the

back pocket of her jeans and threw it on top of the box.

"Bonjour. Uniform and notebook in hand," she said as he walked past her and through the front door that she was holding open for him. Her face remained blank she led him into the snug. "Sorry about the mess but I'm having a clear out." She curled up in a large leather armchair. "Please sit."

Jacques stepped over a pile of papers with a large red tin box on top and took the chair opposite. "Beth, I need to talk to you again about Rob Myers." He looked at her directly. "When I was here on Saturday you said that you last saw Myers the previous Tuesday." He maintained his observation of her and she just nodded in response to his statement. "Since then I've been led to believe that Myers was also here on Wednesday and Thursday. Is that true?"

She toyed with the idea of telling him everything. Absolutely everything. All at once. In one whole sentence if possible, but then… "Yes," she said, her voice low, almost a whisper.

Jacques cleared his throat. "Would you like to tell me what happened on each of those two days?"

Not really. She began to chew her lip. *But I can't avoid it, can I?* She decided to confine herself to only the bald facts and to begin just at the point where Rob had turned up on her porch and tapped lightly on the open front door. "I was in the kitchen when Rob called on Wednesday—"

"Was this by arrangement or did he just turn up?"

She was glad of the interruption. Now she wouldn't have to tell him what she had originally planned for that day. "He just turned up. I wasn't expecting to see him or Will that day. I thought they'd both moved on to Mende."

"Can you remember what time it was when he arrived?"

"It was umm…" In her mind's eye she could see the clock on the oven as she replayed the memory of herself setting the timer for the cooking to complete at seven when she had hoped… *Not now, he doesn't need to know that now.* "Three. It was just after three." She looked straight at him and waited for the next question.

Jacques noted her answer. "And how long did he stay?"

41

"He left about ten past ten, I think." She chewed her lip again. *Please don't ask me why I had to tell him to leave.*

"OK. That's a long time to spend with someone you hardly know. Have you met before?"

"Of course not!" Her response was instantaneous and her tone much sharper than she had intended. She consciously softened her voice before continuing. "He spoke to me on Tuesday," she said. "And then he arrived here unexpectedly on Wednesday."

"So what did you find to talk about for so long?"

Beth thought she detected a note of sarcasm in his voice but dismissed it. "Photography mostly and home and Leeds...and novels," she said as she scanned the spaces on the shelves where Dan's books had been and then the memory of that acutely embarrassing moment jumped back into her conscious. She blinked hard to rid herself of it.

"What about Thursday?" He was sitting back in his chair, watching her closely.

As Beth hadn't admitted that Rob had made a pass at her she couldn't really let Jacques know about the sincere apology he had given her the following morning. "He... umm...just came to say goodbye and to give me his phone number. That's all." Which was true enough but she could feel the colour rising in her cheeks and she was sure it would not go un-noticed by Jacques.

"His phone number?"

Damn. Said too much. "Umm yes..." She thought quickly. "He said if I wanted to get in touch to talk about cameras and photography I could."

Well, that was half a truth. Rob had made it quite plain that, if they did meet up when they were both back in England, he wanted to share more than just a hobby. That was why, as soon as he had gone, she had screwed up the note with his number on it and tossed it in the bin. She forced a smile.

"What time was this?" He was making notes again.

"Five past eleven."

Jacques looked up. "You seem very sure about that?"

42

"I am," she said, but now wasn't the right time to tell him she was putting the place up for sale and that she had been waiting for the Estate Agent to arrive. "I checked my watch immediately after he'd gone. It was five past eleven." Which was absolutely true. Rob's call had been an unwanted distraction and she'd needed to know how much time she had left to make the place look its best.

"And was that the very last time you saw him?"

She nodded.

"Have you heard from him since?"

This time she shook her head.

"Did you see which way he went as he left?"

"No, but he said he was going up to the chateau to get a few more shots of the ruins and the valley and then going to Mende to meet up with Will again."

Jacques made more notes and then paused for a moment. "And there's nothing else you want to add?"

"No."

"And you're absolutely certain there's nothing else you want to tell me?"

She could feel her cheeks burning under his intense gaze. Looking down, she shook her head again.

He closed his notebook and pushed it in his back pocket. "Thank you for your time and I'll let myself out."

She followed him in silence, but only as far as the entrance to the room and, leaning against the doorjamb, watched his receding figure through the long glass panel of the front door as he walked down the path. Just before he turned to close the gate she melted round the doorpost and back into the snug. *What if something has happened to Rob?* She scraped her hair back behind her ears and frowned. *What if I was the very last person to see him? What then?* She looked at all the mess on the floor but her task no longer held any interest for her. She picked up the tin box and slotted it into a space in the bookcase and then dumped the pile of papers on the shelf beneath. Unable to rid her mind of her thoughts she curled up in the chair and laid her head on her knees.

***

The cursor on Jacques' computer screen blinked at him incessantly. *She's holding something back.* He returned to the first page of her evidence for the third time and read it again. *Why would she do that?* He frowned at a typographical error that he had missed, made an amendment and saved the document. *What is it she doesn't want me to know?* In the bottom right hand corner of the screen a pop-up told him he had a new message. He clicked through to his inbox, read the message and then printed out the list of calls and texts made to and from Myers' phone for the last four weeks.

A quick look over the twelve-page document and he had to agree with Will. Myers really did use his phone constantly, which was why, when he looked at the last page and found only two entries for Thursday and nothing since, he finally understood the extent of Coulson's concern for his missing travelling companion.

He flipped back to the first page and began to work through the list, putting a line through all the calls between Myers and Coulson. Considering they were travelling together, there were a significant number of them. A few of the other numbers were French and had been used only after crossing the channel. He would check what exactly they were later, but guessed that they were probably calls made to reserve emplacements on various campsites.

An uncomfortable thought crossed his mind and he glanced at the wall opposite in an effort to dispel it, but couldn't. Sighing, but determined to do his job thoroughly, he got out his own phone and called up Beth's number to see if it was on the list. But it wasn't. Of course, he assumed she was still using the same number she had given him the previous year so he checked his messages. The last one from her had been at the beginning of April. He frowned as he realised that it had been so long since he had last heard from her. And then he recalled that it was Marianne who had told him she was back and not Beth herself and wondered why. He shook his concerns from his mind, focused on the printout and decided he would check out Beth's number anyway.

Lastly, there was a landline number that occurred with some regularity and, working on a hunch and a quick check on the Internet, showed that to be Myers' parents' home. He counted the incoming calls from that number and found that they were almost double the outgoing calls. Jacques grinned. "Well, that looks like a normal adult-son and parent relationship to me," he muttered to no one in particular. On the last page there were a total of seven entries. He thought back to his interview with Will and checked the page again. "There's no text message," he said. "There's no text message recorded for Friday." He looked more closely at the two entries for Thursday and then at the recorded time for each.

Hearing the office door open, he looked over the top of his computer screen as the door then closed again, apparently all by itself. Arms folded he sat back and waited.

"Junior Gendarme Mancelle reporting for duty, sir," said Pierre as he ducked under the counter and presented himself to Jacques. "And Maman has sent you this," he added, carefully placing a small pâtisserie box on the desk.

"Thank you, Pierre." He looked inside and, found a piece of birthday cake. "Happy birthday and I suppose you have lots of presents."

"Come and see," said Pierre darting back under the counter and out into the sunshine. Preferring not to be disturbed at that moment, but not wishing to disappoint the child, Jacques reluctantly left the list of calls on his desk and followed. Outside, he found the youngster astride his brand new red bicycle, a wide grin on his face, and Jacques saw an opportunity.

On the road outside Beth's chalet, Jacques checked that his assistant had everything he needed. "Chalk?"

Pierre patted the left hand pocket of his shorts.

Jacques squatted down and re-set his stopwatch that was

temporarily tied to the handlebars of the new bike. "Ready, stopwatch?"

Pierre nodded his confirmation.

"This time pedal as fast as you possibly can to see if you can reach the path leading up to the chateau. All right, on your marks. Get set. And…" He clicked the stopwatch on. "Go!"

Pierre set off, his legs cranking up and down like a machine, his chest held low over the handlebars and his scrawny little elbows, sticking out like ailerons, sliced through the air. Jacques sprinted up the road after him and checked his wristwatch as he rounded the bend. A few steps further on and he saw Pierre slam on the brakes and jump off his bike just beyond the Sithrez property.

"So, Junior Gendarme Mancelle," he said as he caught up with the boy. "What have you to report?"

A little red-faced and breathless, Pierre carefully laid his bike down on the grass verge and then pointed to a chalk mark in the road with the number 3 beside it. "That's the best so far," he said.

"Well done," said Jacques. He took out his notebook and crouched so that Pierre could see what he was doing. "What we do now is we draw a little sketch," he said as he turned to a new page. "And then we pace out the distances between the three chalk marks." He made a few more additions to his drawing.

"And now we pace," said Jacques striding out from chalk mark three, making a note and then doing the same again from chalk mark two with Pierre beside him having to take more than twice as many steps. He handed his notebook over and let Pierre write in his own results.

With his experiment completed Jacques took the track down past the Pamier farm. "Your maman said you had to be home soon so I will come with you to thank her."

Pierre grinned and chatted all the way back through the village to his own front door.

"Marie, thank you for the cake, and I've brought Pierre back. He has been very helpful."

Madame Mancelle smiled and ushered her son inside. "I'm sorry if he keeps bothering you, Jacques, but he is so set on joining the gendarmerie when he grows up. I'm sure he will grow out of it soon."

"Marie, don't worry, he is not a nuisance and today he has genuinely helped me with my work. So, thank you."

tuesday

Thibault Clergue, a large, bluff man in his late forties with a sometimes annoyingly positive slant on the world, arrived at Gendarmerie Messandrierre at eight as ordered. Jacques briefed him on the poaching case and, as he had expected, Clergue wasn't happy about the need to work split shifts, but agreed in the end. Jacques then informed him about the Myers case.

"This is what I've got so far," said Jacques, laying out a plan of the village on the counter. "Myers left the campsite sometime before or around eleven. I know he called at this property here." He pointed to Beth's chalet on the plan. "He left there at five past and according to his phone records he received a call four minutes and thirty-two seconds after that. The call lasted seventeen minutes and forty-six seconds. That's too long to just leave a voicemail message."

"Who was it from?" asked Clergue.

"It's a mobile number and we do need to check what the call was about." He placed his finger on Beth's chalet on the plan. "So, travelling from here by bike, he would have had to stop to take the call, and in four and half minutes he could have got as far as the Sithrez property. I had one of the boys in the village cycle up there three times yesterday and timed each trip. The shortest distance covered was to here." He indicated a red cross on the plan just before the farmhouse. "So, the area between the dead oak and Ferme Sithrez needs to be searched and, as the path leading up to the chateau runs along the far side of their garden wall, we probably need a detailed search of the ruins as well."

Clergue scratched his head. "Why are we doing this, Jacques? He's a tourist. He's not a minor and he's not

48

vulnerable. There's no suggestion of foul play. So why are we doing this?"

"This is why," said Jacques as he leafed through his file of papers and presented Clergue with the printout of calls for Myers phone. "There are no calls and no text messages after the call at eleven zero nine on that Thursday. That's one reason. The second you can work out for yourself if you look at and consider the pattern and frequency of use. And the third... I gave an undertaking to his companion that I would investigate. And I like to think I am a man of my word."

"OK. But we're not in the Judiciaire de Police in Paris like you used to be."

"Yes, I know that. Just look at the list of calls before you tell me I'm wrong."

Clergue raised his eyebrows and sighed. "All right. You're the boss," he said. "But you do know that Fournier won't be happy if he finds out, don't you? Even if we do find a good lead, he will still haul us over the coals."

Jacques shifted his stance and thought for a moment. "I know, Thibault, and I also realise that there is more at stake for you than me." Standing with his hands on his hips he paused and glanced at the floor before continuing. "I will understand if you don't want to be involved. But I would still value your opinion on whether you think I should pursue this or not."

Clergue leaned on the counter and looked over the first sheet in detail whilst Jacques waited. "I see what you mean about the phone," he said as he flipped over the last page. "But what if Myers has just lost it?" He put down the set of stapled sheets.

"He might have and we might find it when we search the area of his last known whereabouts and that now seems to be here along the top road." Jacques tapped the map. "We think he never made it to Mende, but we don't know that for certain. We have been told that he never made contact with Coulson in Mende but we don't know that for certain either. What we are sure of is that there is no record of Myers staying on the campsite in Mende with Coulson. And we know that Myers has not turned up to start his job in Argelès, nor has he been in contact with the bar owner to explain his absence. He may still have gone to Mende and just not bothered to contact his friend because he had made other plans. And if he did and if he lost his phone there, then it has not been handed in. If someone else has found the phone, either here or in Mende or elsewhere, then, as you can see from the printout, they have apparently not used it."

Clergue nodded. "So we search along the top road then?"

"Yes. And today there is some paperwork to follow up on, the call from the mobile made to Myers' phone, a check to see if Beth Samuels' mobile number is still the same, the Sithrez to interview, and we need to check the woods for traps." He paused as he collected the papers together and mentally marshalled the various tasks into some sort of logical order. "We'll get Fournier his result first and then concentrate on the searches and work on the Myers case."

"Is the poacher Delacroix, do you think?"

"Probably," said Jacques. "And Douffre. He lives in Rieutort. They both did their National Service together and have been up to no good ever since."

Clergue grinned and volunteered for the outdoor duty, as Jacques had expected that he would.

Monsieur and Madame Sithrez were relaxing in the shade on their patio when Jacques called on them later that afternoon. "This is just a routine enquiry," he said as he removed his cap and sat down in the chair indicated.

"Does that mean you will have time for some of my lemonade?" Madame smiled at him. "I made it fresh this morning."

"Thank you." He waited until she had disappeared into the kitchen and then took out his notebook. Since arriving in Messandrierre, the Sithrez had kept themselves a little distant from the rest of the village, but they always joined in with local community events and were generally well-thought of by the other villagers. As he watched Madame go, it struck him that she looked very different from all the other local women. No matter what time of day or night he had seen her she was always immaculately dressed, almost as though she had just stepped off a couturiers' catwalk. He wondered about her age, which he guessed must be late fifties, maybe early sixties, but her perfectly coiffured hair showed not a single strand of grey amongst the deep copper brown hue. But then, some women never really showed their age.

"I'm making enquiries about a missing tourist," he said to Monsieur and handed him the photograph of Rob Myers. "I believe he may have passed by your property on Thursday morning at just after eleven. Did you see him at all?"

Before he could elicit an answer Madame returned with a tray of glasses and a jug of lemonade and placed it in the centre of the table.

"Let me see that," she said, taking the photo and peering at it closely. "Oh yes. You remember, darling, the young man with the phone. He was English, you know." She put the picture back on the table and began filling the glasses and handed Jacques his drink.

"Thank you. Did you learn anything else about him, Madame?"

Clair sat down again, lit a cigarette and took a long pull. Her elbow at rest on the chair arm, she lifted her chin and exhaled slowly as the smoke from the smouldering cigarette drifted into the atmosphere. She smiled at Jacques and placed her cigarette-laden hand lightly on his left knee. "Such a nice young man. I told him we had a liking for English tea and asked him if he would like to join us. Didn't I, darling?"

Her husband nodded.

"And did he join you?" Jacques glanced down and noticed that her nails were coloured the same pale shade of orange as the flimsy scarf that adorned her neck. As she sat back he quickly checked to make sure there was no ash on the trousers of his uniform. Then he sipped his lemonade.

"No, he said he was only here to take some photos of the chateau. Isn't that right, darling?"

Monsieur drained his drink, nodded again and put the empty glass back on the tray.

"Did you see him later that day?"

Madame thought for a moment. "Did we see him later? Let me think. No, I don't think we did, did we, darling?"

"Yes, that's right," he said, speaking for the first time.

Jacques stood up, retrieved the photo and replaced his cap. "Thank you for your help and I'll see myself out."

"Oh, just one question. The boy from Marseille you were asking about last week, has he been found?"

"Yes, Madame. He is safe and with his uncle and aunt."

The walk down the road towards Beth's chalet gave Jacques the opportunity to re-evaluate the case. He looked back at Ferme Sithrez for a moment and realised that, as pleasant and welcoming as the couple were, he never really felt comfortable in their presence. But they had provided some useful information and he now knew that Beth was not the last person to see Rob Myers. Myers had made it to the chateau. However, the search had become imperative, not only of the ruins but also of the deep valley below. If there was a body, as he suspected, it wouldn't be the first time that a photographer had ignored the clear warning signs, climbed over the fence and stood too close to the precipitous edge. Whatever the truth, in Jacques' mind, this investigation now looked like a tragic accident rather then a possible murder. But he sincerely hoped he was wrong on both counts and that Myers was alive and somewhere else in France. After all, the road to the chateau meant that Myers had been heading in the opposite direction from Mende and his agreed meeting with Will.

As he got to Beth's place he saw her struggling with a large heavy box.

"Beth, let me do that," he shouted as he vaulted the low fence and ran across the grass to the porch. "I can do that," he reiterated.

She balanced the box on the arm of the bench. "Thanks," she said as he effortlessly took the weight and lifted it. "If you could just put it in the boot of the car, please."

He smiled and placed the box with ease into the car and shut the lid. When he walked back to her, he noticed the dark marks under her red-rimmed eyes and wondered if she had been crying. "You look tired; are you all right?"

"It's just…" she began, clasping and twisting the fingers of her left hand in her right. "It's just…the Myers investigation…and I did know what you meant when you were last here. I know you think I'm a suspect, Jacques."

He could see the tears welling up in her eyes and taking her hands in his he stilled them and held them lightly. "It's all right," he said. "I now know Myers left your place and went to the chateau. The Sithrez spoke to him after he left here."

She stared at him, her eyes wide and uncomprehending as she thought through the implications of what he had just said. "So…he is safe and sound then?" She slumped down on the bench, relief on her face. "Thank goodness for that. I've been so worried," she said and pushed her hair back behind her shoulders. "Have you spoken to him? He is OK, isn't he?"

Jacques sat next to her, wondering just how much to say.

"I don't know yet. But I do know that on the Thursday he left you were not the last person to see him." He decided not to add the usual 'alive' because of her obvious concern for Myers, and, he blamed himself for some of her distress over recent days. But he couldn't bring himself to tell her what the next steps in the investigation would be and his newfound fears for its outcome. He wanted to save her from that for as long as possible. "The investigation is still ongoing, Beth, but I am sure that I will find him."

wednesday, 3.30 a.m.

The air had the sharp coolness of a clear spring night even
though it was June, and Jacques was less than comfortable
in his combats in the hide he had created. His legs had
begun to ache from being crouched on the soft ground and
the dampness of the earth was permeating through to his
bones. He wanted to stretch and, most of all, he wanted his
comfortable bed and some sleep. At the crack of a twig in
the darkness, he froze and scanned the trees and shrubs in
front of him. He waited and, on hearing a shuffling along
the forest floor, slowly checked the vista again. A large dark
cloud conveniently drifted aside to reveal a partial moon,
and in the beam of the pale ivory light Jacques saw a badger
on his usual nightly patrol for food. He relaxed and settled
down to wait again.

***

Further in the forest, Thibault Clergue was just getting
comfortable in his hide after a call of nature when he heard
what he thought was a fox. Back under deep cover he
watched the small clearing a few metres ahead of his
position. Another sound and he looked to the left. Against
the blackness of the dense shrubbery it was difficult to make
out who or what was there. He waited and listened intently.
On the decaying leaves from the previous autumn he heard
a very careful tread and then a person moved into his field
of vision.

Clergue remained absolutely still. The figure stopped and
looked around and then moved into the clearing. Crouching
down, the poacher paused again to check he was

unobserved. Clergue readied himself. He counted the seconds as he watched the man scrape back the covering of scrub and dead leaves from around the trap. Clergue knew it was empty. He'd removed and, as much as he'd disliked doing so, killed the distressed and badly injured fawn himself when he'd checked the woods the previous afternoon. He'd then deliberately left the trap sprung. The poacher went down on one knee and began re-setting the trap. Clergue emerged noiselessly from his hide and sprinted the few metres to the clearing shouting to the man to halt. Within seconds, Clergue grabbed his prisoner, pulled his arms back and forced him onto the ground, his knee holding him down as he was cuffing him whilst informing him of his rights.

***

The noise made Jacques break his cover and he ran through the trees. He stooped down to help Clergue get the man upright and, shining his torch in the poacher's face, he let out a sigh. "Claude Douffre," he said, "what a surprise! And what about Delacroix? Is he with you?"

Douffre didn't answer.

"Come on, man. I know you two. Where's Delacroix?"

Clergue tightened his strong, massive hand on Claude's upper arm to prompt an answer.

"He's not here tonight. He's drunk."

Jacques shook his head in disgust. He moved the beam of his torch from the prisoner's face.

"Take him to Mende, Thibault," he said. "Get the paperwork done and then get some sleep. We'll scour the woods again later today and on Thursday for any remaining traps and confiscate them."

Clergue nodded and took the route out of the forest used by Douffre.

Jacques set off in the opposite direction to his bed and hopefully a couple of hours of uninterrupted sleep.

The alarm was especially strident and persistent when it rang at seven-thirty. Jacques groaned, rolled over and slapped the top of the clock with the flat of his hand. It was too soon to get up, but nevertheless, he did. From his kitchen he could hear the phone on his desk ringing, but the coffee was too good and too necessary to leave to go cold. Thinking it might be Fournier – it was just like him to ring early – Jacques changed his mind, got up and sprinted through the house to his office and picked up the call.

"Another missing tourist," announced Fournier. "Details by email. Make sure you pick it up immediately." He ended the call.

Jacques stared at the phone, affronted. "Yes, sir," he said and let it drop onto its cradle. Muttering to himself, he wandered back to the kitchen and his coffee. And, as a deliberate act of defiance, which he wished his boss could see, he sat down, added more coffee to his cup, picked up his morning newspaper and started to read.

But his peace and solitude were short-lived. When his office phone rang again, he threw his paper aside in frustration and dumped his half-drunk coffee in the sink.

"Gendarmerie Messandrierre," he said as he walked round his desk to his chair, sat down and listened. "…All right, Fermier Rouselle, calm down…" He reached across and switched on his computer. "…And you're sure it was Delacroix?" Typing in his login and password, he continued to listen. "I really don't see that this is a police matter, Monsieur." He swapped the phone to his other hand, and used his mouse to navigate through to his emails. "…All right. Yes, all right. I will go and see Delacroix, but there is very little that I can do… Yes, I understand that…yes…this afternoon. I will go and speak to him this afternoon." This time the phone landed with a crash as Jacques dropped it onto his desk and let out a deep moan. "That man will have me finger-printing eggs next!" Pulling his chair forward, he clicked on the email from Fournier.

Gaston was smoking at one of the tables on the terrace

outside the bar when Jacques joined him later that afternoon. "You look all in," he said.

"On duty last night and only a couple of hours' sleep," said Jacques as he slumped onto the chair opposite. He moved the empty beer glasses to one side to make room for his notebook, which he opened and put down.

"This looks like official business again," said Gaston, with a pointed stare at the notebook. He took one final puff on his cigarette and stubbed it out in the ashtray.

"More tourists not turning up as expected," said Jacques. He held up a picture of a young man and woman. "Do you recognise these people?"

"Not sure," he said, frowning. Taking the page from Jacques he looked at it more closely and then passed it back. "Got any names?"

Jacques referred to his notes. "Venka Ekstrom and Leif Anderson," he said. "Both from Stockholm."

Gaston thought for a moment and then got up. "I'll just get the book." On his return, he sat down and handed over a record card. "They stayed here for one night four weeks ago," he said.

"Can you remember anything about them?"

"It's a month ago, Jacques. That's a lot of beers!" Gaston threw his hands in the air.

"I know but just try." Jacques noted down the details from the card and then sat back.

Gaston lit himself another cigarette and then ran his free hand through his unruly shoulder-length hair. "No," he said, shaking his head. "I really can't recall much about them, except that I think they were walking and hitch-hiking."

"Can you remember where they may have been going?"

"Home to Sweden, I think, but I can't be sure." He shrugged. "Sorry, I can't help you with this one." He tapped the ash from his Gitanes Blondes and then frowned as though he were searching his mind for a memory. "No, wait a minute. There is something." He stared at Jacques. "Remember that week of rain we had last month when we had the sleet overnight up on the col?"

Jacques nodded.

"Well, if I've got it right, then the Friday they arrived was the end of that week of bad weather and I remember thinking that they just didn't look right."

Jacques waited. "Meaning..." he said eventually.

"I'm really not sure. They had a rucksack each but not much in them. One very small tent, I think." Gaston stopped and thought as he smoked. "I just remember thinking that they weren't really dressed right." He looked at Jacques for help. "They just didn't look right." He shrugged, took another drag on his cigarette and lifted his chin and exhaled.

"So are you saying they were not seasoned campers? Or is it just that they were inadequately prepared?"

Gaston considered the question for a moment. "I don't know, Jacques. They just didn't look like campers, you know. Well, not proper campers. And, if I've got the right couple, then I think she was the one wearing pumps when they arrived here. It had been raining all day, Jacques, and she had pumps on! It just didn't make sense to me."

"OK," said Jacques making a final note. "If you do remember anything else, just let me know."

Gaston nodded. "Are you coming to the fête a week on Saturday?"

"Of course."

"Bringing Beth?" He stubbed out his cigarette and began to collect together the dirty glasses.

Jacques looked away. "Perhaps. I don't know," he said. "The Myers disappearance and she's been...distant. Probably not."

He shoved his notebook in his back pocket and walked into the village and towards Delacroix's farm.

thursday

Beth set out on foot earlier than necessary for her appointment with the Sithrez. At the dead oak, she stopped and took out her camera. Walking backwards and forwards, she lined up the best shots and took a dozen or more. She changed her lens and took some close-ups of the wild flowers around the base and the large knothole in the trunk. With her back to the tree, she gazed at the long view, changed her lens again and took some shots of the valley with the rooftops of the village below. When she checked her watch, she realised she had taken more time than intended and hurried along the top road to the farmhouse.

"Come in," said John, a wide and welcoming smile on his face when she arrived. "We're in the shade on the patio at the back." He stood aside to let her cross the threshold. "Just through there." His outstretched arm indicated a door painted pale green about half way down the short hallway.

Not sure what to expect on the other side, Beth opened the door just wide enough to allow herself to slip through and discovered a large, bright yellow room with a mewing and swarming sea of kittens of every possible feline shade engulfing her feet. She stepped through carefully towards the half open stable door in the wall on the opposite side of the kitchen.

"Hello," she said to the woman outside as she negotiated her way around the back door without letting any of the cats out. "I'm Beth." She stretched out her hand for Madame Sithrez to shake.

Looking up, Madame Sithrez ignored her offered hand and patted the seat of the chair next to her. "I'm Clair," she said. "Do sit down. And I hope you didn't mind the little ones, but it's just too hot for them outside this afternoon."

"No, I like animals." She smiled and, consciously looking over Madame's hair and clothes, wondered why a woman who dressed so carefully and expensively would have any animals in the house at all.

"A photographer, I see," said Clair as she tapped a cigarette out of the packet and lit it.

"Shall I bring the tea and cakes?" John's voice echoed from inside.

"Yes, please, darling."

"Hmm. Yes, well not really." Beth still hadn't been able to decide how to explain. "I've always been interested..." She thought for a moment. "And now that I've got more free time I thought I might try and use my capabilities... umm...more commercially, I suppose." She smiled. "Well, if I can, that is."

Clair breathed out the smoke from her cigarette slowly and then rested it in the ashtray as John appeared at the door holding a large tray. She took the tray from him. "What sort of thing do you mean," she asked.

John slipped out and sat next to Beth.

"Well, I thought I might be able to use some shots for the pictures on cards. Perhaps sell them to a card company or... something."

After setting out the plates, cups and saucers Clair began to pour the tea. "Help yourself to sugar and milk," she said, handing Beth hers. The cigarette, steadily burning in the ashtray at the edge of the table, was infecting the air with its odour as she poured two more cups and passed John his. "Well, I always appreciate a card with a lovely picture," she said, retrieving her cigarette and began smoking it again. "Don't I, darling?"

John nodded and smiled.

"So what sort of pictures are you thinking of using. Are they scenery, still life, objets d'arts...?" She stirred some sugar in her tea and smiled at Beth.

"Anything really, providing it makes a good picture. So the composition needs to be right, the subject appealing."

Debating for a moment an idea that had just come to her she paused. She plucked up the necessary courage and posed her question. "I was just wondering if, well, perhaps you wouldn't mind taking a look at some of the shots I got on the way here," she said, delving into her camera bag. "Perhaps you could give me your opinion. These are just the last few." She handed Clair her camera. "Keep pressing that button there," she said, and then added a tiny amount of milk to her tea. Replacing the milk jug carefully she thought how odd it was to have old-fashioned English bone china in such a traditionally French rural setting.

"They're wonderful," said Clair after only three or four clicks of the button on the back of the camera. Another half a dozen more and she passed the camera to John. "And that view of the valley would make a lovely framed picture for our lounge, wouldn't it, darling? Have you thought about doing weddings?"

Beth was stunned. "No. Yes. Well...not really." She reached for the sugar bowl and took her time about tipping two spoonfuls in her cup. "I have done some wedding photographs but only for a couple of friends and family." She stirred her tea whilst she thought about what to say next. "That was when I was still a student and just after I graduated. I needed the extra money, but then work, life, new husband, got in the way. You know how it is." She shrugged. "So, now that I have more time to...umm...for myself I thought I would see what I could do."

Smiling, she inwardly congratulated herself on having manoeuvred around the sad truthfulness of the past two and half years and made a mental note to remember her words precisely so that she could use the bland and uninformative explanation again.

"Oh, you should. You must. Mustn't she, darling?"

Again John nodded but remained silent and handed back the camera.

"They are very good," Clair said. "Now what about some chocolate cake? I made it myself this morning."

In the loft area of her chalet, Beth was downloading the photos onto the laptop when her mobile rang. She glanced at it and noted only a number rather than a name from her contacts list and decided, initially, to ignore it. A moment later she changed her mind and picked up the call in case it was the estate agent.

"Hello... Oh...sorry, I wasn't expecting..." She listened to the explanation and a furrow gradually appeared on her brow. "Yes, this is still my number... I see... No. No one else uses or has access to this phone... You're welcome, Gendarme Clergue."

Puzzled, despite the plausible explanation given, she stared at her phone as though the answer to the not fully formed question in her mind might appear on the display. But it didn't. Letting out a short, low, gasp of disbelief she turned the phone off altogether and went back to her work.

The download complete she started to sift through the numerous shots, moving the best ones to a separate folder and deleting the ones she didn't want. The various photographs of the valley that Madame Sithrez had liked so much looked far better on the larger screen than she had thought they would and she kept all but two. Choosing between them was difficult but, her decision made, she began to work on the image. She removed two tiny flaws, touched up a couple of the roofs in the foreground, erased a deflated football lying in the valley of the roof of the Mancelle house and very slightly deepened the blue of the sky. Satisfied, she saved the shot onto her data stick and closed the laptop down. She decided she would take it to Mende the next day and get it printed and framed and give it to Madame Sithrez.

She stretched and looked around the loft and groaned. Another room to clear out, she thought. Deciding to do the task now rather then later she pulled open the drawers of the desk and lifted the contents onto the floor, the paper dust causing her nose to itch and run and she sneezed a couple of times. The low bookcase was her next target. She swept her arm across the top and collected all the old hunting trophies together and, still sneezing, took them downstairs and deposited them on the hearth in the snug. She returned with a box and filled it with the books and the contents of the desk and carried that to the snug too and dumped it by the untidy pile of trophies.

friday, may, four weeks earlier

The white van pulled up in Place Urbain V to let out two passengers. Dressed in cagoules and carrying rucksacks, they hurried across the square and took shelter under the veranda of the Drap d'Or pub and watched the driver leave without even acknowleding them. The tables outside the bar were empty apart from near the entrance where an old man with thinning grey-black hair was sitting, a glass of whisky on the table and a cigarette in his hand.

Venka looked at the heavy grey sky. "It's not going to stop," she said. "And that old guy is staring at us. Let's go inside."

Leif nodded and let her lead the way.

Inside, he went straight to a table by the window whilst Venka went to the bar and bought two beers. She put down the glasses, slipped her rucksack off her shoulder and dumped it on the floor. Then, she pulled open her wet coat and hung it over a chair before sitting down next to Leif. "Twenty-two, twenty-three euros and a few centimes," she said, as she counted the money she had tipped out of her purse and onto the table. "What about you?"

Leif emptied his pockets. "Seventeen and some change," he said and then pocketed the cash again.

"That's not even enough for a cheap hotel room," she said, taking a drink of her beer.

"No, we'll have to use the tent again tonight."

"But I'm not roughing it," she whined. "We've roughed it three nights on the trot. I need a shower and I must dry out my pumps. They're still soaked from all that walking in the rain this morning."

"There's a campsite here in Mende," he said, lowering

his voice. "We can stay here for as long as possible and then sneak onto the site later tonight."

"And then get up at the crack of dawn to make sure we leave before the guardian is around." She spat the words at him. "And also no hot water for a shower. With what we've got we can get a train to a larger city and find some work."

"We agreed we would go to St Flour," he said and thumped his glass of beer on the table. "There's plenty of work there and we can stay for as long as you like." He was bored with the argument. He'd been engaged in it almost all day.

"How far is it to St Flour?" Venka's mouth was turned down at the corners and her brow lined with a deep frown.

"About eighty K's," he said. "We can pick up the A75 not far from here and hitch a lift."

"But we could get a train from here and be there tonight, couldn't we? At least we'd dry out." She toyed with her beer glass.

"No, we've got to save what bit of money we have left just in case we need it."

Venka pulled up her wet feet and sat cross-legged on the chair. "What about the other place, the village about thirty K's from here, Messandrierre. It's very small, and it will be cheap. Can't we just head there for tonight and pay for one night's camping?"

Leif sat back, his patience almost exhausted. "No," he said finally.

Venka stared at him but decided not to press him further at that moment. She would wait and try and persuade him later. She groaned, pulled at her scrunchy and ran her hands through her long blonde hair and then re-fixed it in a ponytail. Searching through her coat pockets, she pulled out a slim volume of poems and began to read as the incessant rain continued to flow down the flagstones lining the centre of the square.

sunday, june, the present

It was almost two when Jacques and Clergue walked into the restaurant, still in their overalls, following the morning's search of the ruins and the valley below. There were only a couple of tables vacant and Gaston directed them to one at the back by the window.

"You're late today," he said in greeting as they pulled out their chairs and sat down. "Unfortunately we've no beef left but there is plenty of pork."

Exchanging a look across the table first they nodded their acceptance.

"Can I get you an aperitif?"

"A Sauvignon Blanc," said Jacques. "And if that's Marianne's bouillabaisse that I can smell, bring that as well."

Gaston smiled, cleared the plates from the next table and went into the kitchen.

"So we've found nothing," said Clergue. "But at least I've had a good day in the sunshine and fresh air." He leaned back and grinned.

Gaston came back with two dishes, a basket of bread balanced on top and the tureen of soup, which he left. "I'll be back with the wine," he said and walked towards the bar, collecting and clearing more plates from two other tables as he passed.

There was a myriad of conversations in the restaurant with families and couples dining. Jacques and Clergue were too hungry to talk and filled their soup dishes to the brim.

Gaston put a small pitcher of white wine on the table. Jacques poured them both a glass and downed his in almost one gulp, then refilled it. They both attacked their food and moments later had empty plates.

"So, where does the investigation go from here?" Clergue chewed on his last piece of bread.

Jacques sipped the cool wine and looked round the room. Just about everyone was either waiting for or finishing their cheese or dessert. A hungry look on his face, he gazed at the garlicky stew, glanced at Clergue and then refilled both their dishes. He cleaned the last drop of soup from his plate with a chunk of bread.

"I think we take stock," said Jacques. "In May last year Kellermann disappeared apparently without trace, and no body or any of his possessions have been found." He waited whilst Gaston cleared the plates. "Ten days ago Myers disappears in the same way. That's two disappearances in consecutive years. And now we have the report of two Swedes disappearing who were last seen in Messandrierre five weeks ago, Friday night into Saturday morning."

He looked at his plate of charcuterie and breathed in the saltiness of the ham from the pork butcher in Rieutort. "That's four disappearances in thirteen months, Thibault." Deciding to leave the ham until last he took a mouthful of salami instead and chewed on it. "That's almost Paris statistics and this is a village a fraction of the size of the city."

"Ah." Clergue scraped his fork through a slice of rosette and stuffed it in his mouth. "*Numbers Jacques!*"

The use of his old nickname from his time in the Judiciaire in Paris made him wince and he stared at Clergue. "And how did you come by that?" He felt his left shoulder stiffen and an ache from the gunshot wound scraped across his scapula and lodged in his spine. The distant memory of the thud of the bullet as it hit and the strafing pain as he crashed onto the cold Paris cobbles seared through his mind. He shook his head to rid himself of what had since become his 1.37 a.m. nightmare.

"I was in Chartres last weekend for a wedding, and my wife and your old Capitaine's wife are second cousins. Vuillard was at the wedding, so we had a good, long chat."

Clergue grinned knowingly across the table.

A remembered snippet of conversation surfaced as Jacques recalled his old boss warmly recommending the Cévennes as a good area to police. He'd temporarily forgotten this was where Vuillard's career had begun. Desperately wishing to leave the past where it was he concentrated on his food and finished the plate of meat without looking up or saying anything further.

"Good man, Vuillard," said Clergue, to break the silence. "He had nothing but good things to say about you." He ripped apart the last piece of bread as a broad grin spread across his face. "I think Paris misses you, Jacques."

Emptying his glass, Jacques relaxed back into his chair and grabbed his left shoulder with his right hand and slowly articulated the joint a couple of times. He wanted no more talk of his period in Paris. It was a different time. A different place. A different part of his life. And that was how he wanted it to remain. Unopened. Unchanged and never reconsidered or re-interpreted.

"Lunch is on me today," he said to divert the conversation.

"I accept," said Clergue. "The boss should buy his men lunch from time to time." He slapped the edge of the table and laughed out loud.

Gaston cleared the plates and the empty wine jug and brought the main course. "Some Merlot with that?"

They both nodded and their host returned in moments with a pitcher of red.

"So what are we going to do now about Myers?"

"I'll write up the report of the search." Jacques balanced a fork full of herbed and roasted potato cubes over his plate. "I'll state in conclusion that we are no further forward and that his phone has not been found and that it also has not been used at all since the disappearance. And without any evidence of foul play, or a body or any other leads, I can't see this investigation going any further forward and—"

"And Fournier will tell us to leave it," said Clergue, finishing his colleague's sentence for him.

His mouth full of food, Jacques just nodded.

"And will you let Myers' friend know?"

Placing his cutlery on his almost empty plate Jacques took a deep breath and frowned. "I will have to," he said. "And I'm not looking forward to that conversation." He stared out of the window and thought for a moment and then picked up his fork and stabbed it into his last chunk of pork. His cutlery left untidily on his empty plate, he eased his chair away from the table slightly and wondered what he would tell Beth. He had left her hoping for a resolution that would mean Myers was alive but he still could not be sure of that. Just as he could not be absolutely certain that he was dead, but he knew that the probability was just that.

The restaurant had begun to empty and the noise had subsided to a dull murmur by the time Gaston brought the cheese and left the whole platter for them to help themselves.

"What about the Swedes?" Clergue cut a large chunk of Morbier.

"Much the same as Myers. Seen in a bar in Mende by themselves. The driver of the white van who dropped them off had little to add except that he thought they might have been arguing. Camped here for one night and then nothing. Neither Gaston nor Marianne saw them leave, which isn't surprising because it was a Saturday morning."

Jacques cut another piece of Brie and washed it down with the last of his merlot.

"What I think is curious about the Swedes is that it took so long for anyone to notice they were missing," said Clergue.

"Not really," said Jacques. "Anderson's parents are both dead, a car accident a couple of years ago, and Ekstrom's mother was on holiday in the Caribbean for a month and only realised her daughter was missing when she got home to Stockholm. Venka was due to arrive home two days before her mother, and if there had been a change of plan, Madame Ekstrom was adamant Venka would have let her know."

"Desserts, Messieurs?" asked Gaston, collecting the plates they had used for the cheese. "We have flan aux marrons, mousse au chocolat or tarte tatin."

Showered and changed into his chinos and dark blue shirt, Jacques strode across to Beth's place and found her reading on the porch.

"No uniform." Shielding her eyes from the sun she looked up at him. "Is this a friendly visit?"

"Aren't all my visits?" He smiled at her. Removing his sunglasses, he sat next to her on the bench.

"Not always, well...not recently," she said, placing her bookmark in the page and putting the novel in the space between them.

"I was just doing my job, Beth." Aware that his tone of voice was more unfeeling than he had intended, he softened it before continuing. "And I'm really sorry if that has upset you in any way." He sat back with his right arm resting along the top of the back support.

She smiled weakly. "I do know that...but it was very uncomfortable being a suspect, Jacques. I don't know exactly what it was that you thought I might have done... and I don't think I want you to explain. But the very fact that you thought that I...could hurt someone...that I was a suspect is...was..."

She was looking at him directly, her own eyes were stone cold and he could see how deeply wounded she felt. He wondered if he could ever re-gain her trust. His mind flicked over all those other occasions when he had had been in the same situation, and had had a similar conversation, and he recognised instantly that the outcome of each one had never been in his favour.

He hesitated and wondered if there was any point in proceeding. But he had to know. He lowered his voice to a virtual whisper. "So...perhaps...we can start again?"

She thought for a moment and then almost imperceptibly shook her head. "No, I really don't think that's a very good idea."

Jacques ran his hands through his hair. "Why?"

"I've come back to sell the chalet, and in the next couple of weeks I have to clear the place and then I'll be going home. The estate agent's board is being put up tomorrow."

Leaning forward and resting his forearms on his thighs, he scrutinised the boarding of the porch as he took in her words. "But why are you selling? Why do you want to sell?"

"There's nothing for me here, Jacques. I don't hunt or shoot and I have never had any interest in field sports. This place was Dan's before he met me...and...I came here for the first time last May because I needed to get away from home...and I didn't feel like I belonged here then and...I just don't feel that I belong here now."

He turned to look at her. "All right," he said. "I can understand that. But can't you change that quite easily?" he asked, trying to think practically. "You've already started to clear Dan's things out, so why not replace them with your own."

"It's not that simple, Jacques." She propped her right elbow on the arm of the bench and ran her forefingers back and forth across her forehead. "Yes, the chalet and the deeds are in my name now and I do own it, but the place doesn't feel like mine, and I don't think it ever will. And it was Dan who told me to sell it. It was one of the last things he asked me to do and I promised him that I would." She gave him a half smile. "I'm really sorry that you are having to find out like this. It isn't how I intended to tell you."

Jacques sat up straight. "I don't understand."

Beth sighed. "On Wednesday of last week, when Rob Myers called here uninvited, I was planning to invite you for dinner. I wanted to explain to you properly why I was here and why I was selling the chalet. But it didn't quite work out like that. Rob turned up... He stayed and talked, and I didn't get around to making the phone call to invite you... And it just seemed to have been such a long time since I'd had someone to talk to who didn't know anything about the last two years. And then...Rob disappeared and...

things got complicated…and…"

"Right." Confused and un-nerved, he stood and took a couple of paces away from her. "And you didn't think to ask Rob to leave because you had other plans?" He turned to her, angry.

"Of course," she exclaimed and looked him in the eye. "But…there never seemed to be the right moment and…I don't know…" She averted her eyes.

Jacques stared at the floorboards again and was silent for a few moments. "You didn't tell me you were coming back," he said. "Why didn't you let me know you were coming back?" He lifted his head.

"I didn't want to have to explain in an email," she said in a low voice.

Unable to contain his anger any longer, he moved closer. "All right. Sell the chalet if you must, I really don't care. But I thought we shared something last year that was important to us both." He grabbed her by the shoulders. "Look at me," he said. "I want you to look at me and tell me that last year means nothing to you. I want you to look me in the eye and tell me that all the messages we sent each other since then meant nothing." He was breathing hard as he waited for her answer.

"It was a mistake, Jacques." A tear slipped down her cheek. "It was a terrible mistake. I was in a very dark place and it should never have happened. I shouldn't have let it happen."

He let go of her and turned away. "I don't believe you really mean that, but if this is what you want, then have it."

He strode down the three steps of the porch, stopped and spun round to face her. "But I don't want you to go," he said. Pausing, he made the mental shift to English. "And just to be sure there are no misunderstandings, I don't want you to leave," he said and marched down the path and through the gate.

monday

Beth's night had been restless, troubled and tearful, and when she had eventually fallen asleep it had been fitful. She rose a little after six and wandered into the kitchen to get some coffee and cereal, then she moved into the snug. The place was a mess. The papers and the tin box from last week were still shoved on the bookshelves. Some previously discarded books were scattered in piles across the floor and the box of papers and books from the loft had remained untouched by the hearth, with the pile of hunting trophies in a heap beside it, since Thursday.

As she finished her coffee, she wondered whether to deal with the books first and just keep going until the whole room was cleared and tidy again. It would provide a good distraction for the day. But then there was tomorrow, and the day after and she really didn't want to leave her mind free to ponder her argument with Jacques. She decided to start on the pile of papers on the bookshelf and the stuff from the desk in the loft and to leave the rest as a distraction for another day.

***

"The report on the Myers disappearance is now complete," said Jacques, "and I emailed a copy to you earlier this morning."

"I haven't had time to read it," said Fournier. For once he consciously removed his attention from his own papers and looked at Jacques. "What are the conclusions?"

"That there is no evidence that Myers is either alive or dead. However, his phone has not been used at all since the day of his disappearance. All the usual missing person notices have been posted, but as yet there have been no useful or appropriate responses. The lack of use of his phone, which he did normally use constantly, would suggest—"

"That he has lost it somewhere," interrupted Fournier as he searched through a pile of papers on his desk. "Leave it. There's clearly nothing more we can do." Retrieving what he needed, he looked over the pages in his hand. "You are due some annual leave and I suggest you take it straight away before the holiday season starts."

"Yes, sir."

"And these matters need dealing with." Fournier passed Jacques a handful of files. "Ten o'clock next Monday," he said as he picked up another pile of papers and began silently working through them.

Jacques remained in his seat in front of his superior's desk, hesitating. "About the Myers' case, sir. I think there is more that we can do."

Fournier looked at him, his eyes narrowed. "Do you? I don't. This is not the Judiciaire in Paris. Remember that and get out of my office."

"But if you look at the statistics you will see that four disappearances in this area in just over a year is way above average. We need to delve deeper on all of these missing person cases, sir. We need to question the few witnesses that we do have much more closely."

"And your behaviour is bordering on insubordination, Forêt." Fournier raised his voice. "And I will not have my decisions questioned." With his pen to underline his meaning, he pointed across the room. "And the door is over there."

***

The pile of papers had successfully been reduced to just a few pages which Beth had placed carefully on the coffee table. Everything else, mostly financial statements, spreadsheets, income and expenditure reports from Dan's three businesses, she had shredded and shoved into a black bag. Dragging the bag out of the snug, she shoved it in the bin outside.

Her back aching, she rubbed it as she made her way back to the snug and slumped down in the armchair. She eyed the few remaining pieces of paper. Headed notepaper of quality, she thought as she picked them up. All three letters were equally brief and from the same source with two dated June and the third dated for the intervening December. She carefully looked at the top and tail of each and compared them. Yet again the information was identical and named the sender as Vernier et Fils, a firm of solicitors with an address in Mende. She stared at the three pieces of paper, puzzled. As Dan had regularly used the same firm of solicitors in Leeds, she could not think why he would need one in France, except to handle the purchase of the chalet in the first place. *But that was all settled just after we met.*

And why a payment? What was he paying them for? She re-read the three letters and wondered. Perhaps he was paying the fee for the conveyancing in instalments? But then she immediately dismissed the idea because it had been so unlike Dan to handle business in that way. Still puzzled, she dropped the letters onto the table and sauntered through to the kitchen to make some more coffee.

***

Messandrierre seemed deserted in the late morning sunshine. Jacques parked his bike at the side of his office. He unlocked the door and went in, collected the post from the box and, along with the files from Fournier, dumped the lot on his desk. He thought about making a start on the paperwork, but the clock on the wall was slowly ticking towards twelve, so he went to the kitchen to make his own lunch. He wasn't in the mood to socialise, especially with Gaston. His anger at Fournier was still smouldering and his decision to write his resignation as soon as he had returned was still at the forefront of his mind, awaiting action. On reflection, he decided to consider the idea in more depth over food. After all, if he didn't work as a gendarme, what would he do? And where would he live? The current house came with the current job, a job he was increasingly finding tiresome and unfulfilling. Then he thought about Fournier and his anger re-surfaced as he slammed the kitchen drawer shut.

Well before two he was back at his desk working through the files, some hunting licences that were outstanding, three alleged sightings of Myers that needed to be followed up, some paperwork that needed completing and another missing person report. This was the last of Fournier's files and Jacques paused before opening it. He decided to arrange all the necessary appointments for interviews first and picked up the phone and began dialling.

An hour later he got up and made himself a coffee and, collecting the Kellermann, Myers, Ekstrom and Anderson files from his cabinet as he walked by, he settled himself back at his desk and began reading the new missing person report. Within a minute, he had stopped to make a comparison between the new file and each of the pre-existing ones. He grabbed his coffee, sipped it and sat back. Staring at the grey wall opposite, he let his brain churn through the new and old data. He repeated this process with each piece of evidence from the new file until his phone rang at just after three-thirty.

"Gendarmerie Messandrierre…" He listened carefully. "Where are you? OK… Yes. Don't worry, Marie. I will be there and I'll keep him with me until you get here… No, it is no trouble at all." He picked up the office keys, his helmet, rushed through to the house to collect his spare helmet, stuck his note on the inside of the door and left for Montbel.

He parked outside the École Maternelle just in time for the children to leave and he could not help but smile when

Pierre Mancelle walked out and saw him waiting by the school gate. This wasn't strictly police business, and it wasn't the first time Marie had been in a fix and needed his help to collect the boy from school, but it provided a pleasant interlude amongst the tedium of his day-to-day work. He playfully saluted his young charge as he watched him run across the playground.

"Junior Gendarme Mancelle reporting for duty, sir," said Pierre, skidding to a halt, wide-eyed and smiling, as he saluted in response.

Jacques gave him the helmet to put on. "Your maman is stuck in traffic in Langogne," he said as he made sure his small passenger donned his headgear correctly. "There has been a serious accident where the village road joins the N88 and she is having to sit it out." He checked that the strap was tight enough and then lifted the boy onto the back of his motorbike and got on himself. "Hold on tight," he said and started the engine.

In the cool atmosphere of the gendarmerie, Jacques was back at his desk with his files. Pierre was sprawled on the floor behind the counter with his exercise book, a glass of juice and some bread and cheese whilst the slight afternoon breeze encouraged swirls of dust through the open door. Each was so consumed with his own task that neither one of them noticed nor acknowledged Beth when she first walked in.

"Jacques?"

Startled, he jumped to his feet. "Beth, I'm sorry. I was busy with work. If this is about yesterday…"

She held up her hand to interrupt him. "I'm not here about yesterday," she said sharply. "But I do need your help."

"OK." He noticed how pale her face was and the dark marks under her eyes as he came to his side of the counter. "What can I do?"

"Dan has…had some guns." She looked down at the floor for a moment. "Just a shotgun and a rifle, I think, and I need to dispose of them or sell them or something. I won't take them home because I refuse to have weaponry in the house," she said, avoiding his gaze. Then she frowned. "And I don't know what the rules say about owning or selling guns…either here or at home, so…"

"It's OK. I can help with all of that. There's a shop in Mende that may buy them from you and a gunsmith in Langogne who might be interested also. But I will need to know what sort of guns they are. Can you note down the details?"

She grimaced. "I'd really prefer it if you did that. They're locked away in a cupboard in the boot room and I really don't want to have to…to see them…or to handle them at all."

"OK," he said. "I'll come over later this week and…" She nodded and turned to go but he didn't want to let her leave. "About yesterday…when I come over, can we please talk about yesterday? I said some—"

"There's nothing more to say," she said and escaped through the door.

"But I meant what I said," he shouted after her. Opening the flap on the counter, he fumbled the catch on the half-door and pulled it out of his way and ran out after her. "I really don't want you to leave."

But it was too late, she was gone. "Damn it," he said under his breath as he thumped the wall with his fist and kicked the half-door closed on his way back to his desk.

"Is she breaking your heart, Gendarme Forêt?" Pierre was kneeling on the floor at his feet looking up. "That's what Papa says to Maman." With his left hand on the centre of his chest and his right hand stretched out pleading, he mimicked his father. "Marie, you are breaking my heart, why are you doing this?"

Jacques managed a barely-there forced smile in response, sighed and strode back to his desk. "It's too late. She's already done that, Pierre," he muttered.

"Jacques, I'm so sorry to take so long to get here." Marie Mancelle bustled in through the open door. "But the traffic was impossible and I think the accident must have happened just as I was leaving the village."

Jacques stood and pulled the half-door aside again to let Pierre run through to his mother.

"I hope you have behaved yourself," she said, kissing the top of his head.

"He's been very quiet today and working on his writing for school," said Jacques, collecting Pierre's school bag, exercise book and pencils together and placed them on the counter for Marie.

"And I've had another ride on the police motorbike, Maman."

Marie smiled at him and stroked his head. "Jacques, you must come round for lunch on Sunday. Martin will be home this weekend, so, if you want to bring Beth we can…"

"But he can't, Maman. She's broken his heart," Pierre blurted out.

Jacques stared at the boy astounded, and then looked at Marie who blushed on behalf of her son. Running his hands through his hair, he cleared his throat. "It's nothing," he said quietly. "Perhaps another time for lunch would be better."

Marie nodded, but hesitated, her cheeks still flushed she collected Pierre's rucksack, stuffed the pencils and books inside and silently hurried her son out of the door.

Alone, Jacques marshalled his thoughts and returned his focussed attention to his notes and the files, picked up the phone and called Thibault Clergue in Mende.

"Have you seen the latest report of the missing traveller, Alain Lavoie? Well, have a look at it on the network and call me back as soon as you can. I think we both saw him in Mende on the day of the demonstration."

About five minutes later Clergue called him back.

"OK…and you're certain Lavoie was in the square talking to Delacroix…" He listened and jotted some notes on his desk pad. "…And what time was it when you saw him with Rouselle?" Again he listened and scribbled down a time. "And I saw him with the Sithrez about two hours later." He was listening again… "No, I had the distinct impression that Lavoie was working the periphery of the crowd for handouts and had there not been a sudden surge when he was close to me I would have given him a warning... Mm... Yes... But there's something else, Thibault."

Opening the Lavoie file, he turned to the very first item at the back. "The report of the disappearance has supposedly been made anonymously, but there's too much detail. And..." He turned the report over and looked at the other side. "The person making the report is of no fixed abode. It doesn't add up, Thibault. Lavoie was a traveller, we have witnesses who saw him and talked to him on Saturday, we both saw him ourselves, and then a few hours later a missing person report is filed?" He shook his head and put his foot against the desk. Pushing his chair back to the wall, he listened.

"I just don't buy it, Thibault. There is normally a gap of weeks between when a traveller is last seen and a missing person report being filed. And most often it is a known traveller's body being found that alerts us to the fact that they were missing in the first place."

He thought for a moment. "I think this report is internal and I think it is someone in the local Judiciaire who has put it together. My hunch is that Lavoie could have been supplying information. And that the alleged meeting, for which we have an exact time and a precise location, was with his handler. So, can you do some discreet checking?... All right... Call me if you find anything. And thanks."

tuesday

The faintest of whispers, as light and shifting as a dawn mist, breathed through Messandrierre and across the col to Rieutort when Madame Mancelle phoned her sister-in-law, Annette. Her order for the week's bread and pâtisserie placed, Marie Mancelle could not help but lament the problem of Old Thierry taking the photographs again at the Fête St Jean. "We need someone younger," she said, "with a better eye, you know."

Her sister-in-law was ambivalent at first, but as the arguments presented became more persistent she eventually agreed. Returning to her work, the whisper seeped into the baker's shop as Annette debated the issue over the counter with most of her regular customers.

Meanwhile Madame Mancelle made a second call to her father-in-law, the Mayor.

***

Jacques had decided overnight that Gilles Fournier had to be proved wrong. Handing in his resignation, which he had actually written but not yet posted, was too useful an outcome for his senior colleague. Jacques was certain the man would welcome it and he wanted to remain a difficulty for his boss for as long as he possibly could. He parked his bike outside the Drap d'Or pub in Mende and walked in.

"I'm making enquiries about two missing persons," he said and showed the barman the photos of Venka and Leif. "These two people were dropped off here, on Friday, five weeks ago."

"Yes, I remember and I've already given information to

one of your men." He slid an up-turned chair off the table and put it on the floor.

"I know, but I'm just cross checking the details, that's all. You said there was another man in the pub that afternoon, but that you didn't know who he was. Is that right?"

The barman nodded. "An old guy. That week was my first week working here."

Jacques made a note of his answer. "Has he been in since?"

"No. Not when I've been working." He moved round the table and slid another chair onto the floor.

"And where was he sitting?"

"Outside, most of the time." The barman pulled a cloth from his belt and wiped it across the tabletop. "He was a smoker."

Noting down the extra information Jacques looked round. "Which table and did you notice what time it was when he left?"

The barman thought for a moment and then shook his head. "No, not really. It was very quiet and I was reading the paper. When the couple got up and left I noticed that he had gone also and went outside to clear the table. It was the one by the door."

Jacques leaned against the bar making more notes. "Would you recognise him if he came in again?"

"I'm not sure," he said as he moved to the next table to right the chairs. "Possibly."

Flipping his notebook shut and taking one of his cards from his jacket pocket he placed it on the nearby table. "This is my mobile number," said Jacques. "If he comes in again call me immediately."

He pushed the card towards the barman.

***

By lunchtime the whisper, urgent and seeking an existence on everyone's lips, had become a murmur that was carried on the warming breeze to Montbel.

At the supermarket that afternoon, Monsieur and Madame Sithrez overheard the debate. Listening sympathetically, Madame Sithrez had to agree with the proposal to replace Old Thierry.

"But if not Old Thierry, then who?" was the question echoing back and forth along the valley. Back at her farmhouse, Madame Sithrez picked up the phone and called Madame Rouselle. And the whisper moved through the village again until it reached Marianne in her kitchen at the restaurant and gently propelled her from her ovens to the door of Beth's chalet.

***

Fermier Rouselle was in his barn when Jacques called just after lunch. "If this is about Delacroix," he said, stabbing his pitchfork into a pile of hay and leaving it there, "then you need to know that he's been upsetting my wife again." In height a couple of centimetres shorter than Jacques, he crossed the barn towards him in long urgent strides. "And that fence of his, between his place and my top field, has blown down twice in the last month and each time he's re-erected it he's moved it further onto my land."

Jacques sighed. "I'm here about another matter," he said and pulled out his notebook. "This is Alain Lavoie." He offered a photo to Rouselle.

The farmer moved a step closer, took the photo, glanced at it and handed it back. "Yes, I know," he said.

"Can you remember when and where you last saw him?"

He nodded and wiped the sleeve of his blue overalls across his sweaty forehead. "In the square in Mende on the day of the demonstration."

"And did you speak to him?"

"Of course. I've known Alain for about ten years now. He's a drifter, Jacques. He'll do a day's work for food and a bed for the night and then he moves on."

"Did you offer him some work?"

"I always do." Rouselle sat down on a nearby bail of hay.

"He's a good worker and he was going to come here yesterday to help me with the fencing in the north pasture, but he didn't show up."

"Did you contact him to find out why he didn't turn up?"

The farmer grinned. "You can't contact him, Jacques. Like I said, he's a drifter. He always shows up here in Messandrierre around this time. From here he goes to a farm on the far side of Rieutort. He has some sort of route that he follows every year. In September, he'll be grape picking in Burgundy and then he'll make his way back through here and Mende to Spain for the winter."

"Could he have gone to Rieutort instead of coming to you?"

Rouselle scratched his nose as he thought about the question. "He could, I suppose, but I doubt it. He likes my wife's cooking too much and she always sends him away with what ham she can spare and at least half a dozen boiled eggs."

***

"I see you are selling the place," said Marianne pointing to the 'A Vendre' board close to the road as though it were a complete revelation to her.

"I'm trying to," said Beth. "But getting the French and English estate agents to work together and co-ordinate their publicity has been a little difficult." She ushered her guest into the cool of the snug. "Forgive the mess, but I'm still trying to clear out all of Dan's stuff," she said and, aware that another wave of sadness had hit her, she forced a smile to cover it.

Marianne nodded. "Don't worry. I can imagine how difficult that is. So I will just come to the point. We need someone to take photos at the fête on Saturday and, as Old Thierry is quite frail now, we were wondering if you would like to do the job," she said, a wide winning smile on her face.

Beth was taken-aback. "Umm...I...umm. It's a great

privilege to be asked but I'm not sure I understand what is involved."

"Nothing much, really. There are some official photos of the Mayor for the opening and the presentation of the Hunting Trophies for last season. A few of those are selected for the local press in Mende and a couple of hunting magazines. But mostly it's the attendees who want photos to send to friends and family, which of course you can charge for. We don't expect you to cover all the costs." Marianne waited patiently.

Beth pushed her hair back behind her ears as she mulled over the idea. "Well, I hadn't planned on going on Saturday, but, I suppose I could come for a couple of hours just to do the photos. But who suggested this? And why me?"

Marianne smiled. "The whole village is talking about the wonderful photo of the valley that you framed and gave to the Sithrez."

"So it was the Sithrez, then?"

"I don't know," she said with a shrug. "It was just that the Mayor's office suggested that we use someone new and I thought you might be interested. That's all."

Beth frowned. "Oh right. Umm…right. But I don't have all my equipment here…so depending on the light, the quality of some of the shots may not be that good and I don't usually take portraits either, and…well…umm." Having run out of reasons to say no she grimaced and stopped talking.

"But I doubt that a portrait will present a problem for you if the talk in the village is true."

Beth opened her mouth to speak again but instead remained silent.

Marianne leaned forward. "So does this mean that you will do it?"

At a loss to find any other reasons to refuse Beth let out a gasp. "Of course and…well, thank you."

***

The clear blue morning sky had given way to a vast bank of dark cloud that was rolling in from the north. Jacques glanced up in response to a distant rumble as he stood outside Delacroix's open front door. He knocked and shouted and was about to walk in as Guy Delacroix came round the corner from the back of the dilapidated house.

"Gendarme Forêt," he said. "What is it now?"

"The traveller, Alain Lavoie, do you know him?" Jacques fished out his notebook and the photo.

"Everyone does. He always passes through about now heading north and then comes back at the beginning of October heading south." His explanation delivered Guy gave a disinterested sniff.

"When did you last see him or speak to him?"

Taking a deep breath he shoved his hands to the bottom of the pockets of his overalls. "Saturday in Mende," he said. "I ran into him in the central square. He asked me if I had any work for him and I said I didn't and that if he wanted some decent whisky and conversation to come here about seven. But he said he was already fixed up for the night."

"And you didn't see him or hear from him after that?"

Guy shook his head and then looked at the sky as the thunder cracked and a flash of bright green light striated the advancing bank of cloud.

"Did he say what he meant by 'being fixed up for the night'?"

"No. That was all he said. I supposed he had already arranged food and a bed for the night. But that's what he does, Jacques. A day's work here, a couple of days somewhere else. And all he wants in return is to be fed and somewhere to sleep. Sometimes he will ask for old clothes as well."

Jacques heard the first spots of rain hitting the filthy windowpane as he thanked Delacroix and then turned to walk back up the track to the top road. "And I've checked the car, Guy," he said. "That tax is still outstanding." Stopping where the track met the top road, he stood and faced him. "You have just over a week left," he shouted and

86

waved his notebook at him.

Breaking into a run as the first few spots of rain became a waterfall, he took the steep track down the hill, that by-passed Ferme Pamier, into the centre of the village and just made it to shelter underneath the porch at the church as the storm released its full force. The thunder reverberated through the valley as the lightning serrated the gunmetal sky. There was no choice. He would have to wait this one out.

wednesday

The morning air was fresher and cooler, and the grass covered in heavy dew. when Beth went to open her post box for the first time since her arrival in the village. If she hadn't seen the postman drop something into the box, she probably wouldn't have bothered at all. Strolling back up the path, she sifted through a number of items, some with postmarks from the previous year. Beth only glanced at a hand-written note from the Sithrez, leafed through some local publicity material, noted the letter from the estate agent and then paused as she thought about the letters she had found on Monday. She kicked the front door closed behind her and stood at the foot of the stairs, trying to recall a lost memory. The envelope with the estate agent's name and address on it seemed to remind her of something long forgotten. She ran her fingers across the front of it and then shrugged. Whatever it was, it will come back to me, eventually, she thought as she climbed the stairs to the loft.

On her desk were the three old letters from Vernier et Fils that she had found a few days earlier. Discarding today's post, she picked them up and looked them over again. Well, it can't be business, she thought, as she spread the letters out side by side. *All of Dan's business associates know he died fifteen months ago, and at least another six or eight months before that they knew he was ill and was re-organising his business interests...*

She tapped the desk with her forefinger as she thought through all the possible scenarios. *Unless...of course. That must be it.* She picked up her phone and dialled the number for Dan's accountant and business manager.

"Hi Gerry, I just wanted to check something with you.

It's about the utility bills and local taxes, etc, on the chalet. How do we pay them?" Holding one of the letters she listened. "Right...so, everything, absolutely everything comes direct to you." She stared at the cream coloured page. "...I see...and it all comes addressed to your office? No. I don't need to know the costs." She looked again at the letter and re-read it.

Thank you for your payment of the 15th of June, which has been received and dealt with in accordance with your instructions.

"Yes, yes I'm still here." She desperately tried to think of something to cover her sudden silence and confusion. "Umm...I just wanted to make sure I knew where I could get that sort of information if the estate agents or any potential buyers ask for details, that's all.... What? Oh no... I think I'll be home in another week or so... Yes, I'll let you know. And thanks." She ended the call quickly and sat there chewing her bottom lip as she tried to work out what the payment was for and how much it might have been.

Scooping the letters together, she moved them to the side of her desk and pulled the newly arrived post towards her. The envelope from the estate agent was on top and she stared at it. Something about the quality of the cream coloured paper triggered a thought.

"Last May," she said to herself. "The post from last May..." She ran down the stairs and began rifling through drawers in the kitchen and then the boot room. "Think!" She stood at the breakfast bar. "Think!" Running through her movements in the ten days following the funeral and then the train journey to Le Puy, she remembered. "Of course, it was the Thursday. The day of the storm." She raced back up to the loft and burst into the second bedroom and yanked open the dressing table drawers. In the middle one was an older pile of post, exactly where she had left it.

Back at her desk she looked through the rediscovered post, chucked some advertising material in the bin with a couple of hunting magazines, opened a couple of other envelopes and dumped those too, and then opened another cream coloured envelope – this one clearly annotated with the name Vernier et Fils. The contents were exactly the same as the other three. Lining up the three letters she found on Monday in date order, she slotted the new one in front of them. She took a sheet of paper from the desk drawer and began to note the dates of the letters in one column. In a second column, working backwards and opposite the letter that she had left in the dressing table drawer dated December 2007, she wrote *found May 2008* and immediately underneath that, *Dan's last visit Sept 2007*. The next oldest letter was dated June 2005 and she just added it to the list as she did for the ones dated December 2004 and June 2004. She continued to list the twice-yearly dates in order until she reached June 2000 against which she wrote, *Got married.*

She stared at the two lists, wondering and thinking. She bracketed the dates June 2003 to December 2007 together, drew an asterisk and a linking straight line down the edge of the page culminating in an arrowhead. Against this she noted, *Dan here hunting every Sept/Oct.*

Then she phoned Gerry again but this time it was his office answer phone, so she left a message.

***

"Thibault, come through," said Jacques lifting the counter. "Coffee?"

"No, thanks, I've just come to tell you what I've found out about Lavoie," Clergue said and slumped down on the corner of the desk. "I didn't want anyone to overhear or to leave an electronic trail."

Jacques raised his eyebrows. "This sounds interesting," he said, and sitting back in his chair, he rested his right ankle on his left knee.

"Your hunch was right," Clergue said confidentially. "Lavoie was an informant."

"Did you find out who?"

"No, not really." He folded his heavy arms across his chest. "But everything seems to lead back to Fournier."

Sitting up and pulling the file out of the wire tray, Jacques opened it and turned to the document at the back. "But that's not Fournier's writing," he said as he flipped the sheet backwards and forwards.

"I agree. Apparently Fournier wrote all the details on a plain sheet of paper and asked for the form to be completed on his behalf."

"So, he could be the instigator and therefore Lavoie's handler or he could be protecting a colleague." Jacques sat back and thought for a moment.

Clergue shifted his weight to get more comfortable. "Would Fournier do that, do you think?"

Jacques grimaced. "He's certainly only interested in his own advancement. So, I suppose if it was a senior officer he might see it as useful." Frowning, he inhaled slowly and deeply as he thought about his boss. "No, I think it's more likely that Lavoie was Fournier's nark."

Clergue grinned as an idea came to him. "So we might see a change in his attitude about the disappearances then if you are right!"

"Perhaps." He smiled. "But let's wait and see. Anything else?"

"No. The place they were meeting was listed as a Routier until about 5 years ago. Now it's mostly used by travellers, prostitutes, junkies and tramps rather than bona fide truckers. The place is not very clean and they don't take reservations and, naturally, no-one there recognised Lavoie or remembers whether he might or might not have been there on Saturday evening as planned." Clergue stood up and shrugged. "Exactly what we would expect, Jacques," he said.

"Hmm. And I've nothing useful from Delacroix or Rouselle. They both admit talking to him on Saturday. Delacroix invited Lavoie for a drink on Saturday evening but was turned down and says he didn't see him after that.

Rouselle offered Lavoie work and expected him at the farm on Monday, but he didn't turn up. I still need to see the Sithrez, but, whichever way we look at it Lavoie disappeared some time between three and seven on Saturday and it would appear his last contacts were people from Messandrierre." He stopped and ran his right hand across the day's growth of beard on his chin. "There's something here, Thibault," he said, tapping the files on his desk with his forefinger. "I don't know what it is yet, but there's something. And, whatever it is, it's in this village."

***

It was just before six when Gerry responded to Beth's message. She moved her laptop aside and pulled the list of data she had created towards her before she picked up the call.

"Hi Gerry, thanks for ringing back. I just wanted to cross check some payments made to a firm of solicitors called Vernier et Fils here in Mende... Oh...so you know about them?"

She leaned back in her chair as Gerry explained that the payments were a fixed amount every six months and that the bank had a standing order, which he simply monitored.

"OK, but how much is each payment?" She sat up straight. "Six thousand! Six thousand pounds every six months," she exclaimed. "But that's..." Beth glanced at her list and tried to calculate the total payments from the earliest date to the current year when Gerry interrupted her machinations.

"Right... OK, so the payment is in Euros, so that will be...what...around..."

Gerry supplied the actual amount of £4,998 for the value of the payment made most recently before she could work it out for herself and then continued to explain that as the exchange rate had fluctuated so had the value of the payments in sterling.

She was only half-listening and wanted to crosscheck

something she thought she had just heard but was deflected by Gerry's hurried explanation.

"OK, yes, I get that, but can you tell me when the payments first started and whether there have been any interruptions or not." Beth listened to his next explanation with mounting frustration. "OK that's fine; just call me next week when you've checked all the details. And thanks."

Beth stared at the sheet of paper with her hand written notes for a moment and then, realising she had forgotten to ask one very important question, called Gerry back. It was his answer phone again, so she left a message again.

Unable to concentrate on her work on the photographs, she shut down the laptop and went to the kitchen. She opened the fridge and looked the shelves up and down with no enthusiasm at all and, eventually, let the door glide shut all by itself.

She collected her handbag and went across to the bar.

"Gaston, could I order some dinner to take away for tonight, please?"

"Of course," he said, handing her a menu. He got his order pad from the counter at the back and waited for her to choose.

"I'll have the crudités and the chicken chasseur and one of Marianne's mousse au chocolat, please."

"A good choice," he said, smiling at her and noting her order. "What time do you want to collect it?"

"Is seven OK?"

He added the time to the chit. "And I have an excellent chardonnay that will go with that if you wish."

She nodded and handed over a fifty Euro note. "Gaston, hunting out here in France, what's involved? I mean what sort of costs are there associated with it."

He handed Beth her change. "That depends," he said, walking to the other side of the bar to pick up the wine. "You need a permit to hunt and there are different types depending on where you want to hunt and the kind of animal you are hunting. And the licences need to be renewed regularly. Guns and ammunition can be expensive and most people who hunt have more than one weapon and normally more than one permit." He placed the bottle in a paper bag and put it on the bar.

Gaston stood still whilst he considered her question for a moment, running his thumb and forefinger over his moustache. "So you could easily spend anything upwards from a couple of thousand Euros a year for permits I would guess. And weapons…" He shrugged. "Costs can be from a few thousand up to a few hundred thousand, depending on the quality of the arms." He looked at her and smiled. "Why? Are you thinking of taking up the sport for yourself?"

"No," she said emphatically. "No, no, never!" Cradling the bottle in her left hand, she made ready to leave. "I was just curious, that's all. Thanks and I'll be back at seven."

Back in her kitchen Beth, poured herself a glass of wine and put the bottle in the fridge. Savouring the first sip she nodded her approval. *Gaston is right. He really knows his wine.* Meandering into the snug, she dropped her bag on the coffee table, fished out her phone and called Gerry.

"Hi, its Beth again. Ignore my last message and don't bother with the details of previous payments. But can you just check the date the standing order was cancelled, please? Thanks. Bye."

thursday, october 10th, 1957

Police Constable McKinley bent double as another wave of nausea hit him, and he vomited again onto the wet cobbles of Charlotte Street. Standing up, he wiped his mouth with his handkerchief and took in a deep breath of the damp, smoky air. His stomach empty, he knew he couldn't possibly embarrass himself in front of his new sergeant any further. He pulled his cape straight, replaced his helmet and stepped back over the threshold into the narrow hallway of the shabby back-to-back house. The girl was still in the same place on the stairs, her eyes unblinking and nostrils flared as her breath came short, hard and fast. He attempted a half-hearted smile, but she didn't seem to notice.

"McKinley," his colleague shouted from inside the front room. "All right, lad?"

The young constable nodded and nudged his shoulders back.

The sergeant frowned and took a short step forward. "I've never seen the like of this either, lad," he said in a low voice. "Talk to the bairn. See if you can calm her down enough to tell us some of what happened here." He smiled in encouragement. It was the first time McKinley had seen the sergeant smile.

The iron stench of dried blood mingled with the reek of stale alcohol and tobacco smoke made his stomach flip over in revolt. He swallowed the sensation back and moved out to the hallway. The girl was rocking backwards and forwards, breathing steadily.

McKinley smiled at her. "That's a pretty doll," he said. "I bet she's got a pretty name."

She looked up at him and stared.

Squatting down in front of her, he removed his helmet in the hope it would make him seem friendlier. "Are you going to tell me her name?"

Clutching the doll even closer, the child shook her head and looked away.

Trying a different tack, he moved and sat on the stairs beside her. "And what's your name, then, pet?"

But the girl remained uncommunicative.

"I tell you what. I'll tell you my name if you'll tell me what that pretty doll of yours is called."

Again there was only silence.

Not willing to give up he continued. "Well, I'm Police Constable McKinley, but you can call me Sam," he said. "That's what all my mates call me."

She looked up at him and nodded.

McKinley nodded back. "I bet I can guess your name if I think on," he said.

Her cold ice blue eyes stared at him.

"Does it begin with an A?"

"Guessing games won't get us far, Constable."

The authoritative voice of the inspector on the doorstep made McKinley jump. He stood up with his helmet under his right arm. "Yes, sir."

The sergeant appeared at the doorway of the front room in response to the arrival of his colleague and without prompting launched into a précis of the scene. "Two victims, sir." Glancing at the child on the stairs, he lowered his voice before continuing. "One female, one male. Female is in the kitchen and has been viciously bludgeoned; male over there, sir." He turned and pointed to an armchair in the corner of the room. "Garrotted, sir. Assailant unknown and there's no evidence of forced entry."

friday, the present, st john the baptist fête

"I suppose I have you to thank for organising this," said Beth. She handed her camera bag to Jacques and locked the door behind them. Slipping her keys in her handbag she looked at him.

"I'm happy to go along with the idea if it makes you smile at me like that," he said, his blue eyes shining as he grinned in response. He stepped aside to let her lead the way down the path. It had been late Wednesday afternoon when first he heard about the change of photographer and he had been very surprised by the news. What had intrigued him even more was that, despite his gentle prompting, he had been unable to uncover the name of the person behind the deed. Not that he thought it was a bad thing, on the contrary, he could not be more pleased. As Marianne had pointed out to him the previous evening in the bar, Beth as photographer for the fête was an opportunity not to be missed. And he intended to make the most of it.

Of course, Jacques' employment as a porter for equipment and camera bags had stemmed from Old Thierry's growing use of a wheelchair over the past couple of years. Beth, unfortunately for him, didn't really need his help but he was still happy to do his designated job.

Beth frowned. "So who, then?" At the bottom of the slope they turned and strolled across the car park to the bar and the Salle des Fêtes.

"Does it really matter?"

"Yes, I should like to thank whoever it is."

He thought for a moment and then pulled the door to the community room open. "You might want to wait and see how the evening goes first," he said as Beth walked through.

She stopped and looked back at him, puzzlement across her face.

"I think I would just wait and see," he said. Village politics were murky, convoluted, sometimes strained, and, even after all his time in Messandrierre, often singularly incomprehensible.

Jacques looked around the room. Gaston was behind the bar to his left, Marianne was finalising the arrangement of the Hunting Trophies on the long table by the wall opposite and the rest of the space was taken up by circular tables with eight chairs at each one. Just inside the door was an easel with a list of names of the guests, table by table, and Beth was checking it.

"We're together on table one, along with the Mayor and his wife." She turned to him with an apprehensive look on her face.

"Yes, I know," he said. "But don't worry. They're very nice people." Guiding her through to their table, he placed her camera bag on the floor by her designated place. "Can I get you a drink?"

But she didn't reply immediately and he watched her as she looked about the room.

"Sorry," she said. "I just need to gage the quality of the light in here and check out the possibility of good angles for shots." She pulled her bag onto her seat and began removing her lenses and cameras. "So, I'll say no thanks to a drink. I'm here to work, Jacques, and I suppose I'd better do just that."

Jacques rubbed his hand along the top of his chair and contained a sigh. "OK. Just find me if you need any help," he said. After a moment's pause, with hands in his trouser pockets and head bowed, he walked slowly towards the bar.

Dinner, speeches and the presentations over, Beth finally sat down and accepted a glass of red wine from Jacques. The cheese platter was still in the centre of the table and she hungrily tucked into a large piece of Camembert.

"I've got loads of requests for mounted prints," she said. "Many more than I thought I would." Her eyes were shining as she smiled at him.

"A good venture, then?"

She nodded and took another piece of bread. Her cheese finished, she sat back and tucked a stray tendril of hair back into its place at the side of her neck. "I've been meaning to ask, have you found Rob Myers yet?" She crossed her legs and pushed her chair a little further away from the table.

Jacques cringed. He'd been dreading this question all evening. "No," he said. "But I don't think anything terrible has happened to him either," he lied and tried to cover it with a smile. "Will you be staying for the fireworks later?"

She took a few seconds to think before answering. "Yes, I think I will. So, what is happening with your investigation?"

He realised she was not going to be sidetracked and pulled his chair closer to hers.

"It's still ongoing, and I think Myers' is only one of a series of disappearances in this area since May last year. In each case, the scenario is the same, an individual under thirty-five, usually travelling alone, either coming from Mende or intending to go there, doesn't turn up as expected and there is no…" He wanted to say no body, but decided against it. "No trace of what happened to them. There's no trace of their possessions, in Myers' case, his bicycle and camping equipment, or any of their belongings." Choosing his words carefully, he quietly cleared his throat before continuing. "But in each instance there is a last known contact with someone from this village." He paused and looked at her, but she showed no visible signs of concern at this.

"One of a series," she said as though repeating the phrase would help her comprehension of the issue. "So, exactly how many people are missing?"

"Five…" He wanted to add the usual rider about that number being only the known individuals. For him there was the possibility that there could be more. "Five," he said more definitely. "And in each case there are lines of enquiry that I think have not been fully explored."

"What does that mean?" Her attention fully captured, she put her elbow on the table and leaned her chin on her hand.

"Are you sure you really want to talk about this here?"

He was hoping she would drop the matter but she nodded instead.

"OK. The first disappearance was last May, Kellermann. We have a witness who overheard him speaking English to an elderly couple in Mende. The description of the couple is thin, their height is not known because they were sitting, but they are described as grey-haired, medium build, and that's it."

She looked around. "But that could fit any number of the people in this room, Jacques. The ability to speak English of course will narrow it down a bit, I suppose."

"I know." He scratched his eyebrow and nodded. "For the Ekstrom and Anderson disappearances, the barman at the Drap d'Or pub remembers serving them, and can give us a sketchy description of the only other customer that afternoon, a man with thinning grey-black hair who drank whisky."

"And again that could be half the men in this room. But if he was a regular customer, wouldn't the barman know his name?"

"No, he had only just started work there."

Beth frowned. "That seems like a dead end to me. How can you possibly get anything more?"

"I've been to see him and given him my number and asked him to call me if the same man goes in there again."

"And has he contacted you?"

"Unfortunately, not yet. More precise and detailed questioning at the time could have helped." He shrugged. "It's the same with the other cases."

"So, will you do something about it?"

"I am, but only in my spare time. I've been given specific orders by my senior officer to leave the disappearances alone." Jacques sighed. "He and I don't see police work in quite the same way."

"What will you do, then?"

"I still have to make some enquiries in connection with the last disappearance and then it will be down to detailed checking of all the information collected and maybe some background checks on individuals connected with each case." He smiled at her. "All of which is just routine police work and not very interesting for you," he said and stood up. "Come with me." He gently took her hand and led her through the tables to the middle of the dance floor.

***

From behind the bar, Marianne watched them cross the room and smiled to herself. Catching Madame Rouselle's eye she beckoned her over and the two of them conversed for a few moments before turning to watch the only two people in the room of any interest to them.

Gaston sidled up to the beer pump beside his wife. "Marianne, what have you two been up to?" He pulled a glass from under the counter and began pouring the beer.

Madame Rouselle smiled. "We were just commenting on how lovely Beth's dress is."

Gaston looked from one to the other and then returned his attention to the drink.

"Just girl-talk, Gaston. That's all," said Marianne. And to thoroughly throw him off the scent she turned to Madame Rouselle and moved to another topic of conversation that was circulating the village with a vengeance. "Of course you know Marie Mancelle had Jacques collect her son from school again last week. The boy is always following Jacques around. That woman uses him like an unpaid nanny." Marianne shook her head in disapproval and looked in Jacques' direction again.

Gaston rolled his eyes in response and carried the beer along the bar to his waiting customer.

At table two, Madame Mancelle wore a self-satisfied grin and, leaning back, tapped her sister-in-law on the shoulder at the table behind. In unison, they both looked at Jacques and Beth and nodded their approval.

At table twelve, Madame Sithrez was smoking, despite the clear signs forbidding it, and watching the rest of the room. From time to time, she nodded to some of the other women and passed a few words in conversation, but for most of the evening, her attention had been lavished on Beth. She had been watching her as she easily and smilingly glided around the room with her camera, pausing for shots as required. And, from time to time, Madame Sithrez smiled proudly and inwardly at her new protégé as she worked.

***

It was almost 1 a.m. when Jacques and Beth walked away from the dwindling bonfire and turned up the D6 towards her chalet. The damp air was heavy with smoke and the smell of gunpowder and smouldering wood.

"It feels like Guy Fawkes Night," she said as they strolled side by side in the dark.

"I'm sorry, who?"

"Guy Fawkes. The man who tried to blow up the Houses of Parliament on November the fifth in 1605," she said, grinning at his ignorance of English history. "It's the only time in the year when we have a bonfire and fireworks, along with other traditional things, like cinder toffee and parkin." Seeing his puzzlement she explained. "That's a sort of cake flavoured with ginger."

"I don't understand," he said. "Why would you want to celebrate the actions of an anarchist?"

She turned to him. The look on his face was so incredulous she couldn't help but laugh out loud. "We don't," she said. "But never mind."

"What will you do with the photos of the fireworks?"

"Well, I used different shutter speeds for those so I may be able to get some pictures that are just abstract patterns of coloured light against the blackness of the sky. It will depend how they look on screen when I download them."

They rounded the sweeping bend and without understanding why, she unconsciously matched Jacques' slower pace by shortening her stride whilst continuing her explanation.

"I'll just manipulate them to get the best composition and colour and then decide how to use them."

"This is for your cards that you want to create?" He opened the gate for her to pass through.

"Hmm, perhaps. They could be used for cards with congratulatory messages inside. Or, if they are really sharp and the composition is good enough, they could be enlarged and printed and framed as an abstract picture." She took her keys out of her bag and unlocked the door. "Thanks for your help tonight, Jacques, but it really wasn't necessary."

"I know," he said, putting her camera bag down. "But it has given me an opportunity to spend some time with you and to enable me to tell you again that I really don't want you to leave." She was standing so close she could almost feel him breathing. "Won't you please give me the chance to persuade you to stay?"

She put the flat of her hand on his chest and took half a step back. "Jacques, please don't make this any more difficult than it already is. I will be going home soon so there is no future in this." She looked up at him and hesitated. "There's no sense in…this…us."

He placed his hand over hers and gently squeezed it. "OK," he said. "But can we at least talk about it."

Thinking for a moment, she nodded. "I suppose I owe you that much, at least," she said as she picked up her bag and slipped inside.

sunday

"It's this one," said Beth as she handed a bunch of keys to Jacques. "And I really don't want to stay in here whilst you deal with the guns." She could hear the tremor in her own voice as she was speaking and hoped he hadn't noticed. "I presume they will be loaded and I just don't want to be here," she reiterated, backing away.

"Beth, they won't be loaded. Anyone who hunts never keeps his guns loaded." He opened the outer cupboard. "There's nothing to worry about," he said, standing back and looking at the interior metal doors. "To a man who hunts, guns are not weapons, Beth, but his precious tools. In the same way that a plane is a tool to a carpenter." He slotted the key into the lock, turned it and then stopped. "And you think there's just a rifle and a shotgun?"

Beth nodded and took another step back.

"It's just that this is a very large cabinet and excellent security for just two firearms." He glanced at her. "It's OK. You don't have to stay if you don't want to," he said and pulled open the heavy metal door.

Relieved to be given an excuse to leave the boot room, she immediately turned and was through the doorway. "I'll be in the loft working on the photographs," she called over her shoulder.

An hour or so later, Beth was just adjusting the colour of part of one of the floral arrangements that she had imported to embellish one corner of a photograph of Monsieur and Madame Pamier when she heard Jacques coming up the stairs. "Are they safely locked away again?" She was concentrating on her work.

"Yes. Keys," he said and put them on the desk as he

looked over her shoulder at the screen on the laptop. "That's a fabulous picture. How did you do that?"

"It's very easy with the right software," she said, moving the mouse and making more fine adjustments. "But do you think they will like it or do you think they'll say it's too… umm…arty, maybe?"

"I don't know. The Pamiers' farm has been in the family for almost a century, and the house looks as though it hasn't changed in all that time. So I think, maybe, they are very traditional. All you can do is ask them." He sat on the corner of the desk and made himself comfortable. "But there is something much more important to talk about than the photos from last night."

Beth glanced up at him and, noting his seriousness, looked back at the screen, momentarily unseeing. "I'll just save this," she said as she recommenced moving and clicking the mouse, and then she clicked out of the programme and closed the laptop. Sitting upright in her chair, she waited, wondering if this was going to be the start of last night's promised discussion. A discussion she knew she was not properly prepared to have and one, which she knew in her heart of hearts, she would lose. She mentally braced herself and told herself that her head had to rule her heart. Nothing could come of a relationship that was spread across two countries, two cultures and two languages. Once again, the silent inner voice of her sensible levelheaded self told her such a relationship could not work in the long-term.

"Beth, how sure are you that there are only two guns?"

"That's a strange question," she said to give herself a moment to adjust to the unexpected turn. She paused to think and consider her answer. "I suppose, in truth, I'm not really sure." She sat back and folded her arms. "I know that not long after I first met Dan he told me he had a rifle and a shotgun and asked if I would come shooting with him. I refused. In fact, I stopped seeing him for a while after that."

"And then what?"

"He needed some photos taking of two properties he had renovated in Northumberland, and he asked me if I would do them because he wanted to rent the cottages out. When I'd done that he asked me out again. But I said no because of his liking for guns. That was when he told me he only hunted in France and that he'd moved his guns over here."

"So, it is possible, then," said Jacques, "that he may have acquired more guns in the period when he wasn't seeing you, or whilst he was over here hunting." He looked at her. "Do you think that might be the case?"

She stared up at him in disbelief. "Well, yes, of course it's possible. But he would have told me. I'm sure he would have mentioned it." Her suspicions aroused, she studied his face. "Jacques, what is it exactly that you've found?"

"There are more than two guns," he said. "None of them are loaded, and, as I expected, they have blanks in place and all eight of them are in excellent condition."

Her eyes widened. "Eight! But why would Dan need eight?" Her fear was beginning to tighten into a knot in the pit of her stomach. "I thought there were only two." She could hear the stridency in her voice as the feeling of panic began to rise and to fasten its grip in the centre of her chest. "So who do the rest belong to? They can't possibly be Dan's."

He leaned forward and lightly placed his hand on her shoulder. "Beth, just stay calm and listen. All the appropriate paperwork is in the gun cupboard as well, and they did all belong to Dan."

She stared at him, unable to speak. He lightly stroked her upper arm and, smiling, he sat upright again. "But you will need to demonstrate that you are now the rightful owner in order to sell them," he said quietly.

"But…I don't understand…why would he have so many? Why would he need so many?"

He strode over to the glass-fronted gable-end and stood with his hands in his pockets, looking out across the valley. "Hunters use different weapons for different prey and frequently take more than one gun on a shoot. It looks to me as though Dan really knew his weaponry. There are five 12 bore shotguns, two 16 bore and a rifle. And all of them, apart from one, are English guns," he said as he turned to face her. "That means they will command a very good price if you sell them here."

Still in a daze, her heart thumping against her ribs, she tried to focus on money and numbers. Numbers were easy and she understood them perfectly. "So, a few hundred Euros maybe?"

Jacques smiled and shook his head. "No, probably thousands." He walked part way across the room and stopped. "Well, I'm no expert," he said as he looked down at his shoes. "But I would guess about a hundred and fifty to two hundred thousand. One of them…"

He looked back at her. Her eyes were staring and unblinking as she started to speak but said nothing. Coming back to the desk he stopped and stood opposite her.

"The rifle is a Holland and Holland double," he said quietly.

She felt her breathing stop as she tried to make sense of the information. A heavy frown slowly gathered on her forehead. "I don't understand," she said. "But I think I do know that that's the name of the gun shop in London that Dan visited once where I refused to go in with him."

"You really had no idea, did you?"

She shook her head.

"Beth, you don't have to answer this if you don't want to," he said as he perched on the corner of her desk again, "but why are you so afraid of guns?"

She exhaled slowly, picked up the bunch of keys and locked them in the bottom drawer. She put her head in her hands for a moment to give herself time to decide how much to tell him. "My school friend, Jenny. We were at school together from being thirteen. When we both went on to Leeds Uni we shared a flat in the city." She looked up, and even after this length of time she found she had to steel herself. "It was final exams week. We were very stressed, and on the Thursday evening her boyfriend dumped her. The next day she suggested that we went to her parents' farm that evening for the weekend. This wasn't unusual. We were always at each other's houses when we could be. On the Sunday afternoon I was helping her mum wash-up and, when I turned to say something to Jen she wasn't there. Then there was a shot... We ran out into the yard and round to the farm office. I got there first...but I was too late." She caught a tear from her right eye just as it was about to fall, blinked and looked away.

***

As he walked back to his own house Jacques realised he was developing a growing and distinct dislike for a man he had never even met. Thinking about the source of her fear for guns, he wondered if he was being unjust. It occurred to him that Dan would have undoubtedly known about Beth's appalling experience and may have consciously chosen to keep the details of his cache of arms to himself. If Beth didn't know, he reasoned, she wouldn't be able to worry.

And yet, whilst he could applaud a man instinctively wanting to keep his wife safe and to protect her from harm, he found he could summon little respect for a husband who kept secrets from his wife, especially when those secrets involved significant outlays of cash. When he thought back to the details in the paperwork for the guns, his dislike deepened as he recognised that the second most expensive gun had been purchased just over five years ago, and Beth knew nothing about it.

After letting himself in, he went straight to his office. There was nothing else to do. The hoped-for conversation with Beth had been deflected as, after hearing her explanation of the incident involving her friend, he had decided to wait for a better moment. Switching on his computer, he logged in and began the tedium of background checks on the first suspect on his list, Gaston.

***

"I got your note," said Beth, "and as you can see I've

come prepared." She stood in the yellow kitchen, her camera bag on one shoulder and the laptop on the other.

Clair stubbed out her cigarette in the small dish on the table and smiled. "Some tea?"

"No, thanks. I'm expected at the Rouselles soon so if you could just explain what it is that you want me to photograph, then I'll get on and do it."

Clair gave her a broad smile. "I just thought that it would be nice to have a personal Christmas card this year and we wondered if you would take some photos of the garden for the front of it for us." She looked across at John.

"And the garden is looking lovely at the moment," he added.

Beth did her best to suppress a smirk. She'd always had the opinion that personal cards of this nature were pretentious and now, she never, ever thought about Christmas until December. Her last two Christmases had been especially difficult and she had made up her mind to keep the annual festival to an absolute minimum in future.

"Yes," she said. "Of course, what did you have in mind?"

"Come into the garden," said John as he crossed the tiled floor to the back door. "Leave your bags there."

Beth followed on quickly and saw him disappearing round the corner of the house to her left. Catching up with him, she faced what had once been a small sloping field, now terraced with a series of large raised beds of plants.

"Clair thought here," he said.

Beth looked around and checked the angle of the sun. The field faced mostly south and was bathed in full sunshine. Clair joined them and stood next to John.

"OK. I can see why you have chosen this spot. The flowers are beautiful and will make a lovely background and it's a very sunny part of the garden," she said. "But because this bed is full of plants of various shades of blue and white and you are both wearing blue today, there won't be much contrast between the background and the foreground." She took a few steps back. "I would also like to suggest that we can probably get a better composition if one of you is seated." Beth looked up at the sky again. "I think the best time of day to take the photo would be at about three maybe four in the afternoon when the sun has moved round and some shadow is starting to creep in. It will add more interest and the colours in the flowers and leaves will have greater definition."

She looked from one to the other hoping she had not offended them.

"Half past three," Clair announced. "Come back then and we'll take the photo, and then we'll have some tea and cakes."

Beth smiled. "Tomorrow would be a better day for me," she said. "This afternoon I'm meeting with Marianne to decide which photos are to be submitted to the Mairie and the local papers." She looked at her watch. "And before that I'm due at the Rouselles in twenty minutes, and tea and cakes would be wonderful especially if it could be tomorrow instead."

Clair smiled and glanced at her husband. "Tomorrow, darling, is that all right for you?"

John nodded silently.

***

Late Sunday afternoons in the bar were always peaceful once the last straggle of remaining diners had finally left. Gaston was wiping down the coffee machine as Jacques walked in and claimed his usual stool.

"What can I get you, Jacques?"

"Nothing, thanks. But I need a private word with you," he said, putting his notebook down in front of him.

Gaston glanced at the book and stopped what he was doing. He let out a careworn sigh and pushed his hand through his hair and, with well-practiced precision, aimed and threw his cloth into the sink where it landed with a soft plop. "Is this a private word as a friend or as a policeman?" he asked quietly.

"As a friend..." Jacques hesitated, "...but in connection

110

with a police matter."

"We'd better go into my office, then." Gaston picked up a set of keys and walked out from behind the bar and across the room to a door marked 'Privé'. Jacques waited for the door to be unlocked and then followed Gaston in.

"So what is this about?" Gaston sat behind a small table that served as his desk.

"The Ekstrom and Anderson disappearances," said Jacques, pulling forward a wooden chair and sitting opposite. "I can't ignore the possibility that you may have been the very last person to see them alive."

"I've been questioned about this before, Jacques. By you and your colleagues in Mende. I don't know what else to tell you. Any of you." He pulled open a shallow drawer and fished out his cigarettes and lighter. "Do you mind?" And before Jacques could say no Gaston had a cigarette in his mouth and was already lighting it.

"I know, but I just want to cross-check the details." He flipped open his notebook. "Ekstrom and Anderson were here Friday night to Saturday morning." He looked to Gaston for confirmation.

He nodded.

"Was there anyone else here for Thursday night who might have come across them on the Friday?"

Gaston shook his head and tapped the cigarette ash into the small metal tray in front of him.

"What about the Saturday? Was there anyone who came onto the site before Ekstrom and Anderson left?"

Gaston thought for a moment. "I'm sure there wasn't," he said and then reached across to a stack of three interlocking grey trays and pulled out his receipt book. Finding the right page, he placed it on the table and turned it round for Jacques to examine. "It was when we had that spate of bad weather. The Monteforts left on the previous Sunday, first thing." He indicated the first copy receipt on the page. "An English couple with a caravan arrived on Tuesday and stayed one night." He pointed at the next entry. "And the Dutch couple arrived on Wednesday and left the next day.

111

And this next copy receipt," he added, pointing to the last entry on the page, "this was for Ekstrom and Anderson who arrived on Friday. Saturday was the Forest Walk and I was busy in the bar from early on serving walkers from the village, Rieutort and Montbel who were taking part."

Jacques stared at the page and then up at Gaston. "You know we have no other sightings of these two after they arrived here, don't you?" He kept his eye on his friend to gage his reaction to what had just been said.

"Yes. Your colleagues from Mende made a point of telling me that," Gaston said, angrily stubbing out his cigarette in the ashtray.

Jacques sat back and tossed his notebook down on the table. "Gaston, you have a record and a history of violence. The Investigating Magistrate will be aware of that and it seems that you are the last person to see this couple alive. Are you absolutely certain that there is nothing you want to tell me?"

"My conviction. Yes, that always surfaces eventually. Back then I was hot headed, seventeen and stupid, and I've paid for my mistake." Snapping his receipt book shut, he tossed it onto the top tray. He frowned and looked down. "And, OK, I sometimes get a bit rough with drunk tourists, but that's all…"

"And the fracas at the dance in February?"

Gaston slumped back in his chair. "All right. I got a bit heavy-handed then too. But nothing else, Jacques. I swear."

There was a heaviness to the smoky air in the room and Jacques let the pause in their conversation ferment for a few moments before he stood up. "I didn't put the incident in February on record, Gaston. I ought to have done. But as I was there to smooth things over, I didn't bother with the paperwork." He picked up his notebook. "I hope that doesn't turn out to be a mistake."

monday

As she checked her watch again, Beth berated herself for being so involved in her work on the photographs from Saturday night, and slapped down the screen of the laptop without bothering to save her image or exit the programme. She checked that the charger cable was plugged in and switched on, picked up her camera bag, sprinted down the stairs and slammed the front door shut as she ran down the drive and out onto the road. Half walking and half running, she stopped at the fork to get her breath and then continued at a brisk pace along the top road to Ferme Sithrez.

"I am so sorry to be late," she said as Clair let her in. "I was working on the shots from Saturday and I just lost all track of time."

"Darling, Beth's here," shouted Clair and pushed the front door shut.

"Ah, there you are," said John, appearing from the kitchen. "Kettle's already boiled, so tea will be on the way." He held the door open for the women to walk through.

"Go out to the patio and sit down," said Clair as she collected her ashtray, cigarettes and lighter from the dresser.

"I've got a few ideas for you to think about," said Beth as Clair joined her and busied herself with the usual ritual of lighting-up. "These are just plain paper copies of some examples of the type of prints that we can use to create the cards that you want." Beth laid out some printed sheets on the table. "You can have just a straight photo of you both in various locations in the garden, or if you want something a bit more personal, I can manipulate the images to give different effects. This has a sepia finish, this is straight black and white, and this one is the same but with an added flourish of colour. So you might want that embellishment in the corner to be a favourite flower or plant. This one here adds a more textured look and so on…"

She stopped talking as Clair picked up the pages in turn and started looking at them very closely; her cigarette left burning in the ashtray as on Beth's previous visit.

"Tea and cakes," announced John from the kitchen side of the stable door. Beth jumped up and took the large heavy tray from him and put it on the table.

He let himself out and sat down. "Shall I be mother today?"

"No. I'll do it, darling. You have a look at these and tell me what you think?"

***

In her hurry to get to the Sithrez on time, Beth had left her phone on the kitchen worktop, where it announced the arrival of an incoming call. Switching to voicemail the ring tone went dead and the display changed to show 3 missed calls. A few moments later the mobile rang yet again with a different ring tone and the display lit up to show a text message was awaiting her attention.

***

Alone in the garden some time later, the required shots already in the camera memory, Beth had changed the lens and was taking a series of close ups of the various plants and flowers that John and Clair had identified as their favourites. Intrigued by the colours of some of the petals, the variegation on some of the foliage and the unusual shapes of the plants she had taken many more photographs than were needed.

When she reached the last bed at the top of the field, which had the least amount of planting, but contained a species she had never seen before with dark green stems and leaves and full heads of beautiful dark red flowers, she lined up a close shot. She moved round to the corner of the bed and rested her foot on the edge and took another four photos. Gently re-arranging the foliage near the ground and bending another smaller plant out of the way to take her final shot she froze. On the soil was something she had never expected to see again.

***

Out of uniform, Jacques was taking what he considered to be a well-earned day off and some respite from his demanding boss in Mende. In his small garden behind the municipally-owned house, he was mowing the tiny rectangle of grass that he liked to think of as his lawn and, at first, did not hear the desperate banging on the locked door to his office. At the end of the final strip of faded and yellowed grass he cut the engine, collected the grass box and emptied it as the strange noise reached his ears. When he came round the corner of the garage to the front he found Beth hammering on the door with her fists.

"Jacques! I've found something," she blurted out as she hastened towards him. "You've got to come now. You've got to…"

"OK. OK." It took him a moment to realise she was speaking English and he adjusted his own thought patterns to match hers. "What is this all about?"

"This." She held out her hand and unfurled her fingers. "It was Rob's."

He looked down and frowned, then closed her hand over the object and led her to the terrace at the back of the house. "Sit there and try to calm down," he said.

Back almost immediately with an evidence bag, he held it open. "Just drop that in here." He sealed it and laid it on the table. "I'll make you some strong coffee."

Alone and completely still and silent, Beth stared at the round bed of flowers in the centre of the lawn until Jacques returned and put a mug of coffee in front of her.

"Jacques, this means that he's dead, doesn't it?" She

placed her hand on the evidence bag.

"No." He thought for a moment. He knew he couldn't continue to give her false hope, but he also didn't want her to dwell on that particular outcome. "No, but I think we have to acknowledge that it is a possibility," he said, mentally counting up the number of times he had deliberately deflected her from that conclusion. "Do you want to tell me where you found this?"

Cradling her mug in both hands she stared into the steaming blackness inside. "In the Sithrez' garden," she said.

Jacques nodded. "So, it could have been dropped there by Rob himself or it could have been carried there deliberately or unknowingly by someone or something else." He pulled the transparent bag towards him and examined the contents closely. "It certainly looks as though it has been chewed, probably by a small animal."

He looked at her to gauge her reaction, but she just stared blankly at her coffee.

"Why do you think it is so important?" At first she seemed not to have heard his question. "Beth, we don't have to talk about this now if you don't want to."

He watched as she continued to stare and then, without any prompting, she sat back in her chair. "No," she said. "No, I suppose you'll need another statement so let's get it done straight away, before my courage completely deserts me."

***

The snug was chilly and Beth pulled her cardigan close around her. The rain beat steadily against the window as she wondered what might have happened to Rob.

Jacques will find him. I know he will.

She smiled as she consoled herself with the thought. Then the mental picture of Jacques in his sleeveless tee-shirt and jeans came into her mind. The fine film of sweat on his lightly tanned, muscular arms had glistened in the sunshine as he walked around the corner of the house. She hadn't consciously noticed at the time, she was too concerned with what she had found, but now she relished the memory. But he'll always be a policeman first, she thought. And that realisation was supplanted with another image as she recalled that later, when he had turned to go into his kitchen, she'd seen the scar on his left shoulder. She now remembered kissing it the night of the storm…

STOP IT, Beth. There's no future in this and last year was a mistake. A senseless, stupid, mistake. STOP IT. STOP IT.

Dragging her thoughts back to reality she picked up her mobile and clicked through to her list of missed calls. All three were from Gerry and all within about thirty minutes of each other. Clicking through to her text messages she saw that the only one there was also from Gerry. She opened it.

Standing order hasn't been stopped. All details of payments by email. G.

Beth frowned. *Not stopped? But if it's no longer needed, then of course it must be stopped.* She checked the time and, realising that Gerry would have left his office hours ago, tossed the phone into the armchair opposite in frustration. She would deal with that tedious matter the following day.

tuesday

Thibault Clergue sat behind the desk with Jacques perched on the corner as the postman arrived.

Jean-Paul looked from one to the other as he placed the mail on the counter. "New job, Jacques?"

"Nice idea," he said. "But I'm just taking another day off, that's all." Quickly looking over the envelopes, he sifted out the one personal item – a letter from his father in Paris – and pushed it into the back pocket of his chinos.

"Until tomorrow," and the postman was out of the door to continue his round.

"There's some paperwork to complete and there are some visits to be made. All the details of where, who and what time are in the diary on the PC," Jacques said, handing the rest of the post to Clergue. "There's also Delacroix's car tax. I've given him until the thirtieth to get it sorted. But he was at the fête on Saturday drinking liberally, so I think a little reminder might be appropriate."

Clergue grinned and nodded. "That's a good day's work away from Fournier's beady eyes," he said. "Anything else?"

"No." Jacques checked his watch. "I've got to be at Beth's in ten minutes to meet the gunsmith and then I'll be at Ferme Sithrez and then the Rouselles," he said, collecting his jacket and the evidence bag from the previous day.

Jacques passed the photo of Alain Lavoie to Madame Sithrez. "He was last seen in Mende on the day of the demonstration. Do you know him?"

She shook her head and handed the photo to her husband. "No, we don't know him," she said and then studied the photo again. "But there is something…" She looked at John. "There's something familiar about him, isn't there, darling? Was he the man who asked us for work?"

"Please take a close look, Monsieur." Jacques watched and waited.

"Yes, I think you're right. That's him." John pulled out a chair at the kitchen table and sat down.

"And did you offer him work or anything else?" Jacques turned his attention to Madame again and studied her carefully as she considered her response.

"No," she said and glanced at her husband.

Jacques mentally noted the look. "One last thing," he said, pulling the evidence bag from his pocket and laying it on the table. "Do either of you recognise this?" He stepped back and watched for their individual reactions as they both looked down.

Madame Sithrez spoke first. "No," she said and shrugged, a puzzled look on her face. "I don't even know what it is."

"It's a rakhi, or part of one. A gift given by a girl to a brother or platonic male friend as a promise of life long help and support. Rob Myers was wearing one just like this on the day he disappeared."

Jacques waited for a response.

"Oh, yes, the young man with the telephone, darling, you remember…" She walked over to the sideboard and collected her cigarettes and then sat at the table beside her husband.

"I think we asked him for tea, didn't we?" John smiled as he verbalised the thought.

Madame breathed in the fumes from her cigarette. "That's right, darling." She let the smoke escape into the air as she spoke. "And he said he was in a hurry, darling, and refused our invitation." She pointedly stared at him.

Jacques thought he recognised something purposeful in her voice and manner as she reminded her husband of the outcome of their last encounter with Myers.

Then she turned her wide, smiling face towards her

visitor. "I don't recall seeing the rakhi," she said. "Our conversation with him was very brief."

Jacques hesitated for a moment. He wanted to press them further, but decided against it. He reminded himself that he needed to be careful – he was out of uniform, he was officially taking leave for the day and yet he was in the Sithrez' kitchen furthering an investigation his boss had directly instructed him to leave alone. He decided he'd do some more background checking first. "OK," he said. "Thank you, and I'll see myself out."

It was a short walk to Ferme Rouselle and the farmer's wife was in the yard collecting in her washing. "I think it's going to rain later," she said as she attempted to keep a large white sheet off the ground whilst she folded it.

Jacques immediately caught the bottom corners and followed her in a well-rehearsed pattern of folds. "Madame Sithrez has just told me the same thing," he said, smiling.

"I haven't seen her since the fête. Is she well?" Madame Rouselle put her corners of the sheet up against Jacques', collected the whole thing from him and folded it twice more before dropping it into her wicker wash-basket.

"Oh, yes. She sends her regards." Jacques followed as Madame Rouselle carried her washing across the yard and through the open kitchen door. "She mentioned to me that you helped her find the house here in Messandrierre."

Madame Rouselle beamed as she set the basket down on the table. "That's right. They were living in St Nicholas at the time."

Jacques frowned as he repeated the name. "St Nicholas… I'm not sure I know the town…"

"It's a tiny village in Ariège, close to the border with Spain," supplied Madame Rouselle, still smiling. "They needed someone with local knowledge who could give them detailed information about the property for sale before they committed themselves."

Jacques nodded his approval and pulled out his notebook. "You are a great ambassador for the village, Madame," he said and then sharpened his tone. "I'm actually here on official business." He presented her with the photo of Alain Lavoie. "Can you tell me when you last saw this man?"

Madame Rouselle looked at the picture and then grimaced. "Not since last September or early October. Alain usually passes by round about then."

"Your husband saw him in Mende on the day of the demonstration and spoke to him there. He told me he offered Lavoie some work." Jacques watched her closely.

Madame Rouselle nodded and sat down at the kitchen table. "Yes, but Alain didn't show up as agreed."

"And have you heard from him since then?" Jacques remained standing.

"No. He just shows up when he shows up, Jacques. You never really know when that will be."

Jacques smiled. "OK, thanks," he said. "Is you husband around? I'd like to have another word with him."

"He's in the barn."

He closed his notebook and collected the photo and walked round the farmhouse to the barn at the bottom of the yard. Rouselle, his shirtsleeves rolled up and his hands and arms covered in grease, was working on the engine of an old tractor.

"Jacques, what can I do for you?" He stood up straight.

"This is about the disappearances." Jacques stood his ground and looked Rouselle in the eye. "Lavoie and Ekstrom and Anderson were all heading north according to witness statements, Rouselle. That means they would have walked by this property if they used the top road." Jacques paused to let the implication seep into the farmer's mind. "Someone knows where they are and someone knows what has happened to them." Lowering his voice he took a step closer to Rouselle. "And you were one of the last witnesses to see Lavoie alive. Are you certain there is nothing else you want to tell me?"

Rouselle sighed and thought for a moment. "I've told you everything I know, Jacques. Lavoie didn't show up when expected and I only vaguely recall seeing the Swedish couple. And that is all I know." He reached over and picked up a spanner and turned his attention to the tractor engine again.

The walk back to his office gave Jacques some time to ponder how he could get onto the Rouselle and Sithrez properties and conduct searches without the appropriate warrants, but he soon dismissed the idea. That was too big a risk to take and if he were found out, Fournier would throw the book at him. As he passed by the church another idea came to him and he smiled to himself.

"Perfect," he said and quickened his step.

***

Beth stared at the computer screen.

"...I understand all the details here in your email, Gerry, but what I don't get is why the payment is ongoing." She listened patiently. "So the contract was drawn up by your predecessor and his counterpart here in Mende." Her frustration was beginning to show in her voice and she spat out her next question. "Can't you get copies of the contract and tell me what the payments are for?"

She got up and began pacing backwards and forwards in the space between her desk and the window as she listened to what she considered to be another feeble excuse for not answering her question directly. "Gerry, I just want to know what the money is for and why it has to continue to be paid. Now, if you can't answer that question, then I will ask Vernier et Fils."

Gerry began to dissuade her from doing so. Still pacing, still angry, she listened as she formulated an attack from a different angle.

Staring out of the window, the silence between them was left to grow and fester. "Yes, I'm still here," she said eventually, her tone glacial. "The account, Gerry? Which of the business accounts is funding this payment?... What the hell is that supposed to mean? Of course you can disclose which account. I own them all now."

Beth listened as Gerry dived into another convoluted

explanation. Her anger was soon dispelled by a rapidly growing and overwhelming sense of fear and confusion. "... And it was Dan who set up this other...company with just you and he as the named directors?" She slumped down onto the edge of her desk trying to hold back her tears. Why she wanted to cry she couldn't be sure, but a small droplet escaped and rolled down her face. "I see," she said swallowing back more tears. "Well...I'll...umm...just leave it at that then, Gerry, and thank you."

Stunned, she sat in silence for a while staring out across the valley trying to understand what she had heard. She thought back to the guns. *I didn't know about the weaponry either.* She wiped her face with her hands and moved round her desk and looked at the table of payments. The first one had been in June 2003. She thought back to the Christmas immediately preceding the payment and remembered how overwhelmed she had been by Dan's present, a delicate linked bracelet of diamonds and rubies to match her engagement ring. And then the flush of embarrassment as she recalled how theatrically he had presented her with the ring on Valentine's Day three years earlier, to her complete and utter surprise. Back then, everything just seemed to fall into place and she smiled as she recalled immediately accepting his proposal and his wish to get married as soon as possible. It seemed so right, so perfect, then.

The email on screen was supplanted by the screen saver and she clicked the mouse and re-read Gerry's message. "Hmm, January 2002, that was when he sold those two properties in Northumberland, I think. I wonder if that's where the money comes from."

Her notes and the letters from Vernier et Fils were next to her laptop, staring up at her. Challenging her.

"What else don't I know?"

Looking at the pages as though they would answer her in full she made her decision and with a single, resolute sweep of her hand she gathered up the papers. "But I'm damn well going to find out," she said as she ran down the stairs.

Her mind occupied with her newly found strategy for

getting round Gerry's barrier of confidentiality, she failed to notice Jacques as he strolled up the gravel path to her door. Punching into her phone the number for Vernier et Fils, she began walking through to the kitchen. Jacques' knock on the glass pane stopped her dead. She beckoned him to come in as she waited for an answer. But it was just after twelve and her only response was the answer phone asking her to call back after two. Letting out a deep sigh, she ended the call as Jacques closed the door behind him.

"You seem a bit distressed," he said. "Is everything OK?"

Beth frowned, and realising her face probably looked a mess, wiped her fingers across her cheeks and then ran her hand through her hair. "Lawyers," she said. "How I hate lawyers and accountants."

"Maybe a gendarme can help instead," he said and grinned.

She took a deep breath and, with a calmer disposition, smiled back at him. She wondered why his presence always made her feel so calm, but then she noticed his notebook and dismissed the thought. "Perhaps, but even though you're not in uniform, I see you are here on business again."

"Yes and no," he said, following her into the snug and sitting in the chair opposite. "I need your help," he began as his mobile rang. He checked the display. "I'm sorry but I need to take this."

He picked up the call and moved out into the open plan living area again.

"Gendarme Forêt... Yes... OK. And you're absolutely sure about that? That's great, Will, thank you."

Beth sat forward, curious and a little anxious as she waited for Jacques to return. "Will Coulson?"

"He's just confirmed that Myers did wear a rakhi like the one you found. Apparently, he never took it off."

Beth slumped back into her chair. "So what's next?"

"What's next is where I think you can help me," he said. "If you are willing to." He sat on the chair arm and waited. "It's something very simple and there is no risk for you."

Beth thought for a moment. Now wasn't really the right

time. She wanted to resolve the issue of the continuing payments to the lawyers in Mende and quickly. The possibility of being distracted irritated her. But when she thought about Rob and how tragic it would be if her lack of support might make a difference, she relented and nodded.

"What do you want me to do?"

***

"Marianne, what do you know about the Sithrez?"

"That's an odd question, Jacques." She wiped the bottom of the beer glass with her cloth before she put it on the white paper coaster on the bar and pushed it across to him. "Is this just village gossip or police business?" She stood back, her hands on her hips.

"Both," he said flatly and lifted his beer to take a sip. "Just tell me what you know about them."

"Not that much, really." Marianne leaned her elbow on the bar. "I think when I first met them she said they were from Ariège." She frowned, deep in thought. "I can't remember where exactly but I got the impression it was somewhere near the border. But she is always dressed up to the nines," she said, warming to her subject. "And they mostly keep themselves to themselves. But she is very much in charge in that house. Of that I am certain."

Jacques grinned. *Of course, you would know all about that.* "Do they come in here for a drink or into the restaurant at all?" He began to move his beer glass round and round as he waited for her response.

"Do you know, Jacques, thinking about it, I don't believe I've ever seen them in here or in the restaurant. The village hall for local events, yes." She shook her head and frowned. "In here? No."

"Is there anyone in the village that either of them spends time with that you know of?"

"The Rouselles, I think. I don't know about Monsieur, but she and Madame Rouselle are always on the phone to each other." Marianne stopped and thought for a moment.

"I'm fairly certain that someone helped Madame Sithrez when they wrote to the Mairie asking about moving to the village. The Rouselles, I think. That family has such a long connection to the village that Monsieur Le Maire thought it would be a good idea to put them in touch with each other. Or was it the Pamiers?" She shook her head. "No," she said indecisively. "I'm really not sure now who it was, but it was either Madame Rouselle or Madame Pamier, or was it the old uncle?"

Jacques shook his head, downed that last of his beer and left.

Clergue was just unlocking the office door as Jacques walked down the cow track from the bar. "A good day?"

"Hmm, let's talk, Thibault." He walked behind the counter and automatically slid into his chair, leaving his colleague with the corner of the desk. "The Sithrez said they didn't recognise the fragment of the rakhi. They also acknowledged seeing Lavoie in Mende but denied offering him work or anything else. Rouselle has confirmed that he saw Lavoie but that he didn't show up as expected and Madame Rouselle says she hasn't seen Lavoie since last year. Rouselle is still vague about Ekstrom and Anderson. Coulson has confirmed that Myers wore a rakhi like the one found and Beth is insistent that it is his."

"But only DNA analysis can determine that and without a body we have nothing for comparison," said Thibault.

"I know." Jacques was staring at the wall.

"You do know that you will have to inform Fournier, don't you?" Clergue folded his arms across his wide chest.

Jacques glanced up at him, irritated. "I know."

"You should hand this and the possible new evidence over to the Judiciaire, Jacques. And the sooner the better, for your sake."

He glowered at Clergue. He knew he was right and he knew that as soon as Fournier found out he would suspend him. "Yes! I know," he said, his anger and frustration at his boss' attitude beginning to surface. "But I've come this far and I'm not going to give up." He thumped the flat of his hand on his desk. "Fournier can suspend me and he will, whatever I do. With the additional information, the background checks and the new evidence, I might just as well continue, because I'm already half way up shit creek, Thibault."

His colleague took a deep breath and wiped his large hand across his forehead. "What background information?"

Jacques shot him a glance and then relaxed, relieved that Clergue had not tried to dissuade him from his planned course of action again. "For Kellermann, there is no progress. I think that trail might be stone cold now. I still haven't had a call from the barman at the Drap d'Or in connection with Ekstrom and Anderson, but we have Gaston as the last person to see them and he has an old conviction for GBH. We know also from Gaston that they were heading north so could have left the village using either the RN88 or the top road. If they used the top road, then they would have passed Fermes Delacroix, Rouselle, Pamier and Sithrez. For Myers, we know the Sithrez spoke to him briefly and that he used the top road on the day he disappeared. For Lavoie we know the Sithrez spoke to him in Mende and that Rouselle expected to see him two days after the demonstration in Mende. If he came into the village he would also have been using the top road to go to Ferme Rouselle."

"And we already know that Delacroix is small beer with his string of convictions for poaching, harassment etc.," said Clergue. "Do you think he is capable of…?" He thought for a moment. "Well, what is this crime, Jacques?"

"I know," said Jacques. "That thought has been going round and round in my head too. The complete disappearance of people takes planning and organisation, Thibault. And that doesn't fit with what we know about Delacroix."

"And the others?"

"I still need to run some discreet checks on the Pamiers and some further checks on the Rouselles and the Sithrez. Marianne tells me they came here from Ariège, which probably explains why I can't find anything about them that is more than three years old. But so far the Sithrez are clean."

"You've got to hand all this over, Jacques," said Clergue, getting up. "You do know that a new Investigating Magistrate has been appointed for Lavoie's case, don't you?"

Jacques sat bolt upright. "Who?"

"Bruno Pelletier. And he has been assigned the other disappearances too."

wednesday

Fournier's insulting announcement grated on Jacques and all his muscles bristled with tension. He narrowed his eyes and bit down hard as he set his jaw and willed his anger into controlled, but temporary, submission. "Why Gendarme Clergue?"

"He understands orders and he has a good working knowledge of Messandrierre and its inhabitants." Fournier's tone was harsh and direct. "He will make an excellent local liaison officer for Magistrate Pelletier."

Jacques thought he saw the beginnings of a smirk on his senior colleague's face and his smouldering anger resurfaced momentarily as he mentally acknowledged the implication of Fournier's comments. "Is that all, sir?"

Fournier nodded without even looking up.

In the corridor, Jacques couldn't contain his frustration any longer and as he passed through the fire doors he pushed them so hard they both hit the walls with a heavy thud and then bounced back behind him.

"Bastard," he muttered under his breath as he bounded down the stairs two at a time. "You're an absolute bastard, Fournier." He crashed through the outer door into the courtyard and stopped dead.

"I didn't ask for this." Clergue looked uncomfortable as he leaned against the wall beside his colleague's bike. "I was told only half an hour ago. And if it's any consolation, I refused at first because I thought you would be better suited to the work."

Jacques let his anger subside as a brief, strained smile crossed his face. "Thanks, Thibault, and there's no need to explain. I know Fournier, and I know he took great pleasure in not giving me this particular assignment."

Clergue nodded. "Pelletier wants to talk to you. He's coming out to the village this afternoon."

***

With just under three hours behind the wheel, and probably almost another hour to reach her destination, Beth was growing weary of the driving. Her shoulders were beginning to stiffen and she needed to stretch her legs. She hit the outskirts of Tarascon just as the lunchtime traffic was at its heaviest and the small market town was almost grid-locked. She took the opportunity to stop at a baker's on a corner and bought herself a pain au chocolat. The traffic lights changed to green but the queue of cars continued to crawl across the complicated junction. No one was giving any quarter in the daily race to get home for lunch.

At the southern end of the town, she picked up the route she wanted and turned right onto the D8. By contrast this road was silent and empty as it threaded its way through the high valley. Lush green fields spread to left and right until they butted up against the even higher grey jagged stone peaks of the Pyrenees. Tiny villages with only a few houses in each were dotted along the way. A few kilometres further on, and Beth saw the name board for her destination decorated underneath by a trough of bright summer flowers. She slowed the car and pulled up in a small parking area just outside the church.

The D8 veered off to her left and around the outskirts of the hamlet. It had once riven the place in two and continued straight on past the church, through the few houses and into the tiny central square that contained what would have been the only water supply a hundred years previously. The well, no longer used and liberally decorated with pots of flowers, supported two small seats in the sunshine.

Beth got her camera bag and her coat out of the boot. The sunshine was harsh and bright but the wind blowing down from the Pyrenean peaks was still icy cold. Pulling her collar up, she sat at the well eating her pain and watching the lush grass swaying in response to the breeze. The air was so clear and refreshing, the silence so complete, she wondered why anyone would want to live anywhere else. But then her mind returned to her task and a dark frown crossed her face. She chewed on the last piece of her pastry, screwed up the paper bag and thrust it into her coat pocket.

"To work," she whispered and got up. She checked her watch. It was a quarter to two. "Well, perhaps not quite yet." She resettled herself on the bench to watch the grass grow for a little bit longer.

***

"We have a number of suspects, sir," said Jacques as he brought his update for the Magistrate towards a conclusion. "Kellermann was last seen in Mende with a couple who are thought to be English tourists. And we have nothing after that. If he did come here, he didn't stay on the campsite, and we know that from checks made at the time. Ekstrom and Anderson were last seen alive by Gaston, the campsite manager, and there is a vaguely-remembered sighting by Fermier Rouselle, but again, nothing further. Lavoie was last seen in Mende and spoke to three of the village inhabitants on that day. He was expected here by Fermier Rouselle who offered him work and has stated that Lavoie did not arrive as expected. His wife has confirmed this and has said she last saw Lavoie towards the end of last year. We know that Myers was last seen alive by the Sithrez, but searches of the area where he was last sighted have delivered nothing until the day before yesterday when a fragment of a rakhi, said to be his by two separate witnesses, was found in the Sithrez' garden by Beth Samuels."

"And Samuels was your original suspect in the Myers disappearance, yes?" Pelletier's soft northern voice made Jacques blench as he was reminded of her possible involvement.

"That's right, but…" He took a deep breath and reached down and unlocked the bottom drawer of his desk. "But there's something else." He placed a large evidence bag on the desk in front of them. As he carefully stretched out the corners, a handgun, a silencer and a scruffy brown cloth could be clearly seen through the transparent plastic. "On the Monday of last week, Madame Samuels came here to ask me for help with the disposal of her deceased husband's hunting weapons. I visited her on Sunday to examine the guns and to make an inventory. On Madame Samuels' behalf, I then visited the gunsmith in Langogne and, when I presented him with the details of the weapons, he agreed to take them all. The gunsmith and I met at Madame Samuels' chalet first thing yesterday. Whilst I was emptying the gun cupboard I found another small, locked recess that had been completely obscured by a stock of ammunition when I made the inventory. This pistol was in that recess."

Pelletier removed his rimless spectacles, narrowed his eyes and fixed Jacques with a penetrating stare. "Did Madame Samuels know it was there?"

Jacques thought back to his conversations with Beth when she had been his only possible suspect. If he was going to change her mind about leaving and get her to trust him again he couldn't afford for her to become a suspect a second time. And he certainly had no wish to be her interrogator again. He glanced at Clergue, who stood behind Pelletier, in the hope of some support, but Clergue remained motionless, his face blank. Jacques decided to be completely open with the Magistrate.

"I don't know, sir. But I doubt she had any idea it was there. When I made the list of guns and told her what was in the cupboard she was visibly shocked and upset. She has a complete phobia of weapons. That was why I thought it best to get the cache of arms out of her way as soon as possible."

"So," the Magistrate looked up from polishing one of the lenses on his handkerchief, "you didn't question her about it when you made your discovery?"

Clergue raised his eyebrows and Jacques knew he would

have to admit his past involvement with Beth. But how to say it was his difficulty. He wanted to stay in Pelletier's favour in the hope that he might be able to remain on the periphery of the investigation if not directly involved. He decided to be honest but chose his words carefully. "It would not have been appropriate for me to question her, sir."

Pelletier replaced his glasses and, sitting forward, he rested his elbows on the desk and immediately picked up on the telling statement. "Appropriate for you personally or appropriate for the investigation?"

Jacques knew the truthful answer was 'both' but took a less incriminating stance. "The investigation."

"Ah." Pelletier sat back and smiled. "At least you have the decency to be straight with me, Forêt, and I appreciate that." He turned to Clergue. "Our first interview will be with Madame Samuels," he said. Rising from his chair, he picked up the evidence bag containing the gun.

"Magistrate Pelletier," said Jacques, also standing. "I think there are a few more things you need to know before you undertake that interview."

"Go on."

"All eight of the weapons in Monsieur Samuels' gun cupboard had the appropriate accompanying paperwork from the original date of purchase, including receipts for payment, up to and including the very last licence renewal before his death. The documents needed for the export of the first three of the guns from England had also been kept and filed. As have the export documents for each of the four subsequent guns that he bought in the UK. The eighth gun was bought here. There were also receipts for all of the stored ammunition. Monsieur Samuels was a meticulous record keeper, which is why I believe the handgun can't be his. That was the only weapon that had no attendant paperwork of any sort. Not even the original receipt for payment."

The Magistrate frowned and crossed his arms. "And your point is what?"

133

"All Samuels' weapons were hunting guns, they were all in excellent condition and the only ammunition stored was that required for those guns. Whilst I acknowledge that men who hunt will also sometimes buy handguns and use them for sport, I have never yet come across a situation when a hunting man might need a silencer for such a gun. My suggestion would be that he may have been storing the weapon for someone else."

Pelletier sat down again. "Or that he had a use for it himself and that was his reason for hiding it. Do we know anything about Samuels' background?"

"English businessman from Leeds, that's a large city in Yorkshire, sir. Married in June 2000, I think, and was fifteen years older than his wife. No children." Referring to a page of notes on his desk, Jacques paused briefly and then continued. "He has owned the hunting chalet here in the village since 1996 and was a regular visitor each September and October to hunt and always came here alone. He's clean as far as we're concerned. I can find only one record for a parking fine being imposed in Mende when he was last here and he settled that immediately. I haven't had chance to check with the British police yet."

"Ah." Pelletier stared at the handgun for a few seconds and then stood. "I worked with Vuillard on a case some years ago and he said then you would go far. It's a shame you did not continue in the Judiciaire. Fournier may not appreciate your capabilities, Jacques, but I do. Unofficially I want you to work with Clergue and me on this. Find out what you can about Samuels. Clergue and I will see Madame Samuels, and then you can get this checked for fingerprints and matches with any open cases," he said, addressing the last instruction to Clergue.

"Madame Samuels is not at home today," said Jacques hoping that he would not be required to explain how or why he could make such a bold and convincing statement.

Pelletier smiled and nodded. "Ah," he said. "But she's not returned to England, I hope."

"No, sir. She's just out for the whole day." Jacques

returned the Magistrate's penetrating stare.

"Good. Until we know all we can about this handgun and the reason for it being stored at her property I think I will be asking her to remain here no matter what her original plans were."

Jacques watched as his colleague and the Magistrate left the gendarmerie. He sat at his desk and let Pelletier's words echo through his mind. Beth being required to stay had some compensation, but it was not how he wanted things to be between them. He wanted her to choose to stay. He wanted her to choose him. But he still hadn't told her about the handgun and he knew he could not let her find out about it for the first time from Clergue and Pelletier. He fished out his phone and sent Beth a text.

Dinner at mine when you get back. Text with eta. J

***

"I'm looking for some old friends of mine," said Beth as she approached the lady behind the counter of the Mairie. Having rehearsed what to say for most of her journey in the car her confidence seemed to wane and the butterflies in her stomach would not be stilled. "I know they live in the village somewhere," she ploughed on, "but I've lost their full address and I was wondering if you could help me find them. I've got some pictures here." Beth took the cover off her camera, clicked through to the shots she wanted and passed the camera across the small counter.

The woman at the Mairie studied the photos and then shook her head. "No, I'm sorry I don't recognise anyone," she said. "But I've only been here a couple of years. If you go to the church and ask Père Martin I'm sure he can help you."

Beth thanked the woman, left and walked back through the village to where she had parked her car. The narrow streets of old houses provided some interesting subjects and her photographer's eye could not let such an opportunity go by so she took a few moments to collect more images.

The church of St Nicholas was small with a rounded tower, opposite the only entrance, which contained a tiny altar bathed in light from the three stained glass windows above it. The sun was in just the right aspect to harlequin the stone floor with colour and she captured the moment with half a dozen shots. The stone walls were pocked with damp and what little remained of the faded and worn murals was barely visible. Beth was conscious of her kitten heels clattering on the flagged floor and stepped down the nave as gently as possible. To her left was a dark oak door that led to the Sacristy and she knocked. When there was no response she tried the handle, which gave way to her touch. Inside the room was dark, damp and empty.

Out in the sunshine again she stood in the doorway and looked around and to her right, behind the church was a small graveyard. She followed the narrow path between the headstones, stopping a couple of times to read the ones that caught her eye and to take photographs. In the furthest corner of the walled area, the priest was on his knees weeding the edges of an old gravestone, his shock of bright white hair glistening in the sun as the breeze blew through it.

"Père Martin?" Beth held out her hand in greeting.

"Yes." Standing with difficulty and using the headstone to steady himself once upright, he removed his gardening glove and took her hand lightly. "Madame, do I know you?"

"No, but I've been told that you may be able to help me."

The old man smiled, leaned against the wall for support and took off his other glove and dropped it on the ground next to his discarded trowel.

"I'm looking for some old friends of mine and I've lost their address but I know this is the village where they live and, as I was in the area, I thought I would try and find them." Beth took out her camera and clicked through to the shots she wanted. "This is a photo from a while ago, maybe you recognise them," she said, showing the screen to the priest.

Delving into the pocket in his cassock, he pulled out a pair of wire-rimmed spectacles and peered closely at the back of the camera. "I'm not sure." The puzzlement on his pale and wrinkled face was quickly replaced with a wide smile. "My house is just there and I like a lemon tea in the afternoon. Come, we'll talk over tea," he said and deftly led the way through the headstones to a gate in the wall a few metres away. As she followed she stopped for a moment to take some long shots of the cemetery and captured a picture of a large granite headstone flanked by a pair of angels, heads bowed in prayer.

"This way, Madame," called the old man as he held the crumbling iron gate open for her.

In the cool of his small and untidy house, she perched on the edge of a rickety dining chair, afraid to allow her full weight, as slight as it was, to rest on the tall back. Père Martin placed a cup of lemon tea in front of her.

"Now the pictures," he said reaching for her camera and peering closely. "Of course, yes. Monsieur and Madame Pamier." He smiled and nodded and, letting the camera rest on the table, he continued. "They're not here any longer, you know, but I can't quite remember how long ago it was when they left." Sitting back he gazed up at the ceiling. "Must be over two years now," he said. Then a frown crossed his face. "Yes, it was something to do with illness in the family, I think."

Beth sipped her tea. "And you're sure there's no-one else in the other photos that you recognise?"

The old man looked at her wearily. "I can't be certain, Madame," he said. "My eyes aren't what they used to be and my memory plays tricks on me these days. But what I do remember is that the Pamiers left round about the same time that Juan De Silva stopped coming to the village." He swirled the piece of lemon around in his cup.

Beth waited patiently for him to say more.

"I'm sure it was at the same time because there was a rumour in the village that he had gone with them to…" He stopped and thought, his brow creased in a desperate effort to recall some lost detail. "Alas, I can't remember where it was they went to now." He finished his tea. "Nice people," he added. "And Juan worked for them, on and off, for about four years, I think. A very caring young man. Not of the greatest intelligence, you understand, but caring and considerate."

He stopped and smiled as he recalled a long forgotten thought. "And a very gifted artist." He got up and ambled across to an old, well-used bureau full of disarrayed papers, yet he seemed to have no difficulty in finding what he wanted. "A very gifted artist," he said, coming back to his seat and putting a pencil drawing of the village in front of her.

Beth picked it up and had to agree. "That's stunning," she said. "The detail is incredible and the perspective is perfect. I couldn't take a photo as good as that!" She handed it back and the old man gazed at it lovingly for a moment.

"What about the name Sithrez, Père Martin? Does that mean anything to you?" Beth pushed her empty cup away from her.

"Sithrez?" The old priest looked blank for a moment and then sat up straight. "Gone, Madame. All of the family, long gone." He relaxed back in his chair and into a reverie of his time at St Nicholas. "A lovely parish, this, you know," he said. "I've been here almost sixty years…a lifetime… "

Beth listened and let him talk at will until she felt there was nothing further that he could give her and then she waited until he fell back into another short silence before excusing herself and leaving.

***

Beth slumped down in one of the two well-worn but mismatched armchairs as Jacques handed her a glass of wine. "I don't know if anything I've found out today will help you at all," she said, resting her head on the chair back.

"There will be something," said Jacques, placing his half empty glass on the wooden mantelpiece between a pile of letters and a mug containing the dregs of cold coffee that he realised had been there for two days. "Even if it is only one tiny detail that allows us to eliminate someone from the investigation it will be something." The barbecue fire spat and crackled, and he moved back out to the patio in response.

Beth looked around the small dim living room, the external wooden shutters at the single window and the patio doors providing the only privacy. In the corner some shelves were untidily crammed with books and papers, and the old fashioned wallpaper showed signs of once being covered with numerous pictures. "Your house looks so lonely," she sighed as she kicked off her shoes and stretched out her toes.

"What? Come out here in the sunshine and tell me about today." The charcoal hissed and smoked as he moved the food around the griddle.

"Your house," she said, padding across the polished wooden floor and past the table, carefully set for the two of them and with a slim vase of flowers at one side, at the furthest end of the room overlooking the tiny garden and the patio. "It seems so lonely." She leaned against the window frame and sipped her wine. "Just like the chalet. Not really lived in. Only ever used when required."

She handed Jacques his glass.

"Perhaps." He finished his wine and put the glass on a small wooden table and then turned the kebabs. "The house goes with the job, so it's not really mine anyway." He looked at her and smiled. "Well, not for much longer. I'm thinking of leaving the force."

Beth stared at him. "Why? Why would you do that? You love being a policeman."

"Not really." His attention focussed on the cooking he failed to notice the short stunned silence.

"I don't understand."

"Investigation is what I love, Beth, not policing," he said and offered her a bowl of olives. "Not finding lost bicycles and settling disputes between farmers and babysitting the

Mancelle boy." He stopped what he was doing and thought about what he'd just said. "Pierre is a nice boy and, if I'm ever lucky enough to have a son of my own, I would like to think that I would be as good a parent as Marie is." He smiled and turned back to the fire. "But what I do here? That's not investigation. Some of it is not even police work, it's providing a community service, which, of course I am happy to do. But it's not investigation and I realise now that I should never have left the Judiciaire in Paris, and I shouldn't have hidden myself away down here in the sticks."

Beth hesitated. "Are you going back to Paris?"

He looked at her. Her face had lost its colour, her expression was numb and he could sense her unease. "I don't really know," he said. "But the pace of life is much easier down here and perhaps if I had a reason to stay…"

"A reason to stay?"

She was frowning again and he decided not to pursue the matter further. "Come on, let's eat," he said, piling the skewers onto a large platter. "Sit and eat and tell me what you've found."

"I spoke to the local priest and showed him some of the long shots of the room from the fête." Beth spooned a pile of salad onto her plate. Picking up a kebab she began pulling chunks of chicken from it with her teeth and continued her update between mouthfuls. "At first he wasn't sure if he recognised anyone at all." A forkful of salad halted her discourse. "But when he looked more closely he did eventually recognise the Pamiers," she said attacking the skewer again. "He started telling me about them."

Beth helped herself to another piece of bread and ripped it in two. "They'd been in the village for some years and then suddenly left," she said, chewing on a chunk of bread. "Then he said that he thought they still owned the house they had lived in at the far end of the village. And then he mentioned, almost as an aside, that there had been a disappearance there a few years ago," Another kebab made its way onto Beth's plate. "This food is delicious, Jacques.

Did you make the kebabs?"

He shook his head, "I can look after myself but I'm not that good," he said grinning. "Marianne made them for me. So what else?"

"Oh, yes. He gave me the name," she said as she used her fork to scrape the contents of the second skewer onto her plate. "And I also made some notes when I got back to the car. But the interesting thing was that this person disappeared around the same time the Pamiers left St Nicholas." She looked up. "What?"

Sitting back in his chair, his food hardly touched, Jacques grinned at her. "You have a mighty appetite for someone so small."

"I'm starving. It was a long drive there and back, you know."

Jacques poured some more wine. "OK. Eat and keep talking then." He pulled his chair closer and spooned some salad onto his own plate and began to eat. "Tell me about the disappearance."

Beth frowned, her fork half-way to her mouth, "Oh yes, Juan de Silva was the name Pere Martin gave me. A beautiful artist if the drawing I was shown was anything to… " She looked across at Jacques. "What's the matter?"

His face lined with deep concern he let his fork clatter onto his plate as he dropped it. "That name." He shook his head. "There's something I should remember about that name." Drumming his fingers on the edge of the table he bowed his head trying to recall something from the very back of his mind. He scraped his chair back and ran through to his office.

"Juan de Silva," he said brandishing a file a few moments later and sitting opposite her again. He shoved his half-empty plate out of the way and dropped the file onto the table and opened it.

"Traveller, aged twenty-seven." He rapidly leafed through the pages. "Reported missing in November 2007 by his mother in Spain. Referred from Spanish police to Ariège and then to us." He looked up.

Beth was staring at him and it took him a moment to realise that he had been talking to her as though he was briefing one of his colleagues. He cringed at his crassness.

"I'm sorry." Reaching over he placed his hand over hers. "This is really good work, Beth. For the first time in weeks I've got a lead that might make a difference."

Beth pulled her hand free and took a sip of her wine. "You say you're thinking of leaving the service, Jacques, but from what I've just seen, you'll always be a policeman first."

Her words stung him and, in that silent moment, he realised he had probably lost her again.

Alone in his office, the only light from his computer screen, Jacques made one last change to the words on the page and then clicked the icon for print. He smiled to himself as he thought about how Fournier's anger would erupt when faced with finding a replacement for him in the middle of the peak holiday season. Collecting the letter from the printer he re-read it and then hesitated.

Back at his desk, he watched the digital clock in the bottom left-hand corner of the screen register 00.24 a.m. He pinched the bridge of his nose as Beth's accusation echoed through his conscious.

Always a gendarme.

He frowned and wondered why he could not get things right with her. Available women were simple, and just that, available.

Why is it the ones you especially want to spend some time with are always so difficult?

He sat back and stared at the monitor and, having decided that if he wanted Beth in his life then he had to make room for her, he logged out and switched off.

His attention returned to the letter. *No, there really is some justice in the timing of this.* Wielding his pen, he scrawled his signature at the bottom, folded the page, enveloped it and sealed it. He would casually drop it onto Fournier's desk at his next meeting without even bothering to let his boss know it was there. On the front of the envelope he wrote "G FOURNIER" and stabbed a full stop at the end of it.

thursday

Beth set the tray of mugs and coffee on the low table in the snug. "Please help yourselves to milk and sugar." She noticed for the first time the strange package covered by a man's handkerchief at the other end of her table.

"Thank you. I'll get straight to the point, Madame." Pelletier leaned forward and, keeping his eyes on Beth, snatched the cover from the evidence bag. "Do you recognise this?"

Beth recoiled. "No." She swallowed and stared at the handgun for a moment. "No, I've never seen it before and I don't allow guns in the house."

The Magistrate nodded to Clergue who stepped forward, removed the weapon and returned to his place behind Beth's armchair.

Pelletier sat back and savoured his coffee. "You say you don't allow guns in the house, and yet I am told that there is a large gun cupboard in the property."

"Yes. But the guns have been taken to Langogne to be sold. They were my husband's. He used to come here to hunt every year." Beth pulled a bunch of keys from the pocket of her dungarees and placed them on the table. "These are Dan's keys," she said. "Take them and look for yourself if you like."

The Magistrate smiled. "The firearm I've just shown you was found in your gun cupboard, Madame. Can you explain how it got there?"

Beth frowned. Her mind in confusion, she pulled at her hair and began twisting it. "I…umm… No."

Jacques' advice about keeping calm and just answering any questions truthfully and directly coursed through her mind. *How much more stuff like this can there be?*

She came to a decision. "Umm… All I can tell you is that Dan bought this place before we were married. I knew there was a place for him to store his guns here because he told me, but I did not know until very recently how many weapons were in there. I haven't seen that thing before and I don't recognise it and I do not know how or why Dan had it in his cupboard."

She laced her fingers together in her lap and stared at the Magistrate.

"Why would you think I would need your husband's keys, Madame?"

The chill in the man's voice made her shudder. "Yesterday evening, Gendarme Forêt told me that you were taking over the investigation for Rob Myers' disappearance and that you would be here this morning to talk to me. He said you had found some new evidence and that you might wish to make a search of the property and possibly the gun cupboard." She stared her interrogator straight in the eye. "That was all he said. New evidence. He never said it was a gun."

She tightened and released her fingers against her knuckles constantly as Pelletier watched her through lowered eyelids for, what seemed to Beth, an interminable amount of time.

His coffee finished, he returned his mug to the tray, picked up the keys and then spread them out on the table in front of her. "Can you tell me what all these keys are for?"

"Front and back door at home, window lock, garage and shed at home," she said, pushing each one aside as she named it. "Garage and chalet doors and desk drawer here, this large one is for the gun cupboard and these last few are Dan's office keys at home. He had an office above the card and stationery shop that he…that I now own in Leeds."

The Magistrate looked above Beth's head to Clergue. "And you are sure there is only one key for the gun cupboard?"

Beth nodded and waited for the next question. *How much*

more? I can't tell you things I don't know.

"Does anyone else have a set of keys for this property or the gun cupboard?"

"No." Beth scraped her hair back behind her ears. "Sorry, that's not strictly an accurate answer. Umm, the chalet first. I have my own set of keys and when I came here to put the place on the market I brought Dan's keys with me because I knew I would need to hand them over to the estate agent. At the moment, the agent has my set of keys. There is only one key for the gun cupboard and that's it," she said, lifting the large steel key off the table.

"Has there always been only one key for the gun cupboard?" Pelletier was watching her again.

"Yes… I think so." She searched her mind for anything that Dan might have said that could help her to be more certain. Frowning, she looked away, uncomfortable under the Magistrate's stare. "Dan never indicated, as far as I can remember, that there was more than one key to the gun cupboard."

"Can you describe the gun cupboard?"

She let out a sigh. "There's no point," she said, her voice spiked and strident. "You can see it for yourself. It's in the boot room on the other side of the kitchen. A full-length wooden cabinet on the left. The guns were kept inside there."

She offered the bunch of keys to Pelletier. When he wouldn't take them, she dumped the whole lot down on the table and ran her hands through her hair. "It's just an ordinary looking wooden cabinet…just like a kitchen cabinet, I guess. I've never looked in it. I've never wanted to look in it."

"Alright." Another nod to Clergue and Pelletier stood. "Thank you, Madame, and Gendarme Clergue will take the keys and examine the gun cupboard if you don't mind."

Beth nodded.

"We may need to talk to you again," said Pelletier. "So please let us know if you are intending to leave for home."

"You're right," said Pelletier as he strode into the gendarmerie and stood in front of Jacques' desk. "Madame Samuels knows nothing and she was visibly repulsed by the sight of the handgun."

He turned to Clergue. "Get the weapon to ballistics and checked for fingerprints, etc. When we get those reports, if there is nothing to link it back to the chalet or either of the Samuels then we can tell Madame she is free to travel home when she wishes."

Jacques scowled at his computer screen and clicked the log out icon. He knew the reports requested would be rushed through and could be available as soon as late afternoon the next day or Saturday morning and Beth could be gone by Monday.

"You need to be aware, sir, that you will find my fingerprints on the edge of the silencer. When I lifted the gun out of the recess and opened the cloth the silencer rolled out of my hand and onto the floor. I had no evidence gloves with me at the time."

Pelletier nodded. "If Madame is cleared, I expect you would like to tell her the good news."

Jacques gave his colleague a half smile. "Yes, sir, and thank you."

The Magistrate perched on the edge of the desk. "Your research? What have you found?"

"There's the possibility that this case is much larger than we ever envisaged." Jacques pulled out from under a pile of papers and files in front of him a large sheet on which was printed an outline of France with each département defined. "Here in Ariège between 2003 and 2007, six people disappeared, apparently without trace. All with a final link to the village of St Nicholas." He used his pen to pinpoint the location on his map. "St Nicholas is very similar in size and population to Messandrierre and we believe that both the Pamiers and the Sithrez lived there, but these connections are still to be investigated thoroughly." Moving his pen to the opposite side of the country he continued. "Over here in the Vercors there were five disappearances between 1999 and 2001, similar circumstances to our cases and those in St Nicholas."

Jacques moved his chair back and waited as the Magistrate took up the map and considered the new information.

"And your advice, if you were running this case, would be?" Pelletier folded his arms and looked at Jacques over the top of his spectacles.

A wide grin on his face, Jacques stood up and nodded towards Clergue. "That myself and Gendarme Clergue work on the local cases and continue to search for and gather further evidence and that you look at the wider picture and make contact with our colleagues nationwide and perhaps enlist another junior officer to handle your paperwork and the finer details of any research you need."

"You're wasted here, Jacques. Vuillard would take you back in an instant, you know, if you were interested, that is. I'll be in my office in Mende. Keep me updated." He folded the map, slotted it into his briefcase and left.

"What next, Jacques?"

"For you, ballistics and forensics, and for me..." He picked the letter addressed to Fournier out of his wire tray and stared at it.

"Regretting your decision now?" Clergue stepped forward.

"No. Not for a moment." He propped the envelope up against the monitor on his desk. "I was just debating with myself whether two weeks was enough time to bring this to a proper conclusion."

"And is it?"

Jacques grinned and nodded.

***

"What a lovely place you have," said Clair, stubbing out her cigarette. "The view over the valley is breath-taking,

148

isn't it, darling?"

As usual John just nodded.

"And you want to sell! I can't believe you're selling the chalet."

Beth smiled and tucked into her scone, liberally covered with jam and cream. "I have no real use for the place. And I have things...work at home that needs attention. Not to mention my new venture of the cards," she said, holding up the folder of prepared pictures that she had completed for her guests.

Clair helped herself to a piece of cake. "Oh, but surely you could keep the house and just visit every other month or so for a couple of weeks at a time, couldn't you? Are your work commitments so heavy that you have to be there every day?"

Beth smiled and wondered how someone who knew her so little could somehow pinpoint a solution that she had herself consciously and deliberately avoided. "No, there's a business manager in place who takes care of most things but —"

"There you are, then," said Clair, an open smile on her face. "Let the manager manage." She reached over and poured herself some more tea, her numerous bracelets clinking together on her wrist. "We could have such lovely afternoons together here, drinking tea and chatting, couldn't we, darling?"

"Perhaps," said Beth. "However, there's work here to do too, and these are the final selection of proofs for the cards you wanted." She handed over a file. "Have a look at them and tell me how many cards you want of each design. If you can let me have your response by Sunday evening, I will get the cards made up here or at home and send them on to you. I'm really hoping that I can leave in the next day or so and once I know that I can then I will finalise arrangements with the removal firm."

"We will, won't we, darling? And before I forget, I've got some bramble jam for you." She dropped the file in her basket and took out a jar covered with a circle of bright red gingham and a handwritten label on the front. "I thought you might enjoy it with your toast for breakfast."

"Bramble jam! I love bramble jam, and do you know, I haven't eaten that since I was a child? And we have a couple of scones left," she said, looking at the plate on the table, "so let's share them and try the jam now, shall we?"

"That's very kind," said Clair. "We have plenty, so save this. Save it for a day when you can have a long and peaceful morning all by yourself and then indulge."

***

"Madame Pamier, have you and your husband always lived here in Messandrierre?" Jacques stood in the chill of the windowless and low roofed outhouse despite the offer of a small three-legged stool.

"No," she said. "We've moved about quite a bit because of my husband's previous work. It was when his uncle became too ill to run this place that we moved here and took on the farm."

Jacques watched with distaste as she eviscerated the chicken lying on the large wooden butcher's block. "So, that would be how long ago?"

The sea of feathers on the floor rippled as she moved across to the stone sink and rinsed her soiled hands. "Just over two years ago, I think." She let the cold water run as she thought for a moment. "Yes. It was late in 2006 when my husband's uncle had the first serious heart attack and we came over for a couple of weeks at first. Then just after Christmas, Paul, my husband, came back to live here and work the farm, and I came a few weeks later once I'd organised the removals." She nodded and then looked at Jacques. "So we've both lived here since February 2007, at first with Paul's uncle. He was only with us for a few months after that. A massive stroke," she said, wiping her hands on a grubby cloth.

"I'm sorry to hear that. Just one last thing, Madame, do you know this man?" He showed her the photo of Lavoie.

150

She peered at the picture, lips pursed and her eyes giving nothing away. "No," she said after a moment.

"And what about these two?" He now held out the pictures of Ekstrom and Anderson.

"No." Again her face conveyed nothing. No emotion at all, not even the slightest spark of curiosity.

"Perhaps you could look more closely. They were in the village at the end of May and could have passed along the road at the top of your property, Madame."

She glanced at the photos again and shook her head. "This is a working farm, Gendarme Forêt, I haven't time to stare out of windows and watch out for passers-by."

"And what about this man?" He held up a picture of Juan de Silva. Madame glanced up and Jacques saw hers eyes suddenly widen as she looked at it. "Do you recognise him?"

She looked away, her face a blank. "Yes. He used to help out on the farm."

"This farm?" Jacques was watching her even more closely.

She kept her eyes on her hands as she tied and trussed the chicken. "I can't remember. I haven't seen Juan for a few years now." She picked up the bird and her knife. "Is that all? As I said, this is a working farm and I have many things to do."

She moved past him and out into the yard.

Jacques acquiesced and followed her, promising himself he would do some more background checking. The reaction he had just seen convinced him that she may know more than she was telling.

friday

The street in Mende was quiet as Beth walked slowly towards the offices of Vernier et Fils. The building was Napoleonic in design with large pillars at the entrance and the gilded plaque, portraying Liberté above, unmistakable evidence that she was in the right place. Her stomach began to churn and she turned back striding out towards the end of the road and then stopped. She looked in the window of a mobile phone and IT shop, her eyes darting from one product to another without really seeing any of them. Taking a deep breath, she pulled her jacket straight and examined her reflection in the window. She smoothed her hand over her hair and walked back to the Notaire's office. This time she went in.

"Madame Samuels?" The young woman at reception was polite but distant. "Follow me, please." She led Beth up the stairs and into a small room on her right and left her there.

Beth smiled at the only other person in the room, a well-dressed woman a few years older than her. Unbuttoning her jacket, she sat next to the window to wait, for what, she was not entirely sure. Desperate to keep her mind a blank, she gazed down on the small park on the opposite side of the road.

"It's Madame Samuels, isn't it?"

The sound of English being spoken after almost a month of virtually nothing but French confused Beth for a moment but brought her attention back into the room.

"Yes, it is."

Looking at the woman more closely, she noticed her dark brown eyes had a hardness to them and that her heavy make-up could not quite hide the shadows underneath. Her lipstick was just a shade too bright and too red, and the dark roots of her bleached hair were just beginning to show. "Have we met before?"

"No. I'm Veronique Devereux and I'm the reason you're here."

"I'm sorry but I don't understand." A realisation began to creep into Beth's mind. Or perhaps it had always been there. That strange niggling fear, the denied dread, so long lived-with, that her trust had been betrayed and that this woman was the living and breathing embodiment.

"There's no easy way to tell you this…"

"I can imagine," said Beth, iciness glazing her voice as she watched Madame Devereux closely. "But just say it anyway."

"I'm the mother of Dan Samuels' son."

"A…son." She swallowed hard and remained motionless but unnerved. "Dan has a son?"

Voices from past disagreements and conversations about having children bombarded her thoughts and a tear drizzled down her face. The seemingly endless tests to find out what was wrong, the research into the use of IVF and the numerous heated arguments between them. "A son…" She wiped her hands across her cheeks as more tears flowed. "How old?"

"It was over before he met you," Veronique said, avoiding Beth's piercing stare. "That's what you really want to know, isn't it?"

"So the payments…" It wasn't really a question, or even a statement, just a verbal expression of something that she reluctantly admitted she had unconsciously acknowledged to herself after her last conversation with Gerry. But now, as she ordered her thoughts and tried to take control of her feelings, speaking it made it real, undeniably real.

"…are for—"

"Don't tell me his name!" Beth twisted her ring round and round her finger. "Sorry. I…umm…I didn't mean to shout at you. I'd rather not know the personal details," she added and thought for a moment. "But there is just one

153

question. When we got married in June 2000, did Dan know he had a son then?" Beth was still, her hands clasped together in her lap, steeling herself for the worst.

Veronique lifted her chin and looked at Beth through narrowed eyes. She didn't answer immediately.

Beth prompted her. "Well, *did* he?"

"I'm not going to lie to you," she said, her tone a little more conciliatory. "I think there have probably been too many of those already. No, he didn't know then. But he found out about his son by accident seven years ago and he has seen him whenever he has been here hunting. But I want you to know that I never asked for anything. I never wanted anything from him and it was Dan who insisted on making the payments."

Beth nodded. He would, she thought. *At least that is what the man I thought I knew would do.*

"Of course I know that Dan is dead now, and if it is your wish that the payments stop then I will accept that," she said, her voice flat as if to underline the prosaic French practicality of her attitude.

Beth thought for a moment, "I can't stop them," she said. "The terms of the agreement are such that there is a fixed end date and the only qualification is if the funds run out before that end date."

She stopped to consider if she should say any more. Dan had managed all his businesses and assets exceptionally well. She could leave Madame Devereux wondering and anxious if she wanted to, but, in the end decided on complete honesty. And yes, she had to agree with Veronique on that single point, honesty was clearly something that had been lacking for a very long time. "And that's unlikely to happen," she said quietly and fixed the other woman with a stare. Taking a deep breath to rid herself of the distastefulness of the conversation, Beth stood. "Thank you for meeting me and I wish you and your son the best for the future."

"Wouldn't you like to meet my boy?" Veronique rose and took a step towards her.

Beth shook her head. "I…no…I don't think so," she said and moved towards the door.

Veronique hesitated momentarily. "I would like to ask a question also," she said. "I know that Dan is dead but I don't know how or why." She looked at Beth. "If it's too difficult to talk about, I'll understand," she added almost in a whisper.

Tears were pricking the back of Beth's eyes again. "He was diagnosed with an inoperable brain tumour and a few months later he was gone. His deterioration was rapid and vicious and painful and I…umm." Tears were streaming down her face as she struggled to continue. "But I was there," she said. "Through it all, and at the end I was there."

Beth yanked the door open and ran down the stairs and across the road to the park.

***

The barman at the Drap d'Or nodded in recognition as Jacques walked through the door. "The table by the window," he said as he wiped a damp cloth across the surface of the bar.

"And you are sure he is the man who was here at the same time as the Swedish couple?"

The barman shrugged. "I'm as sure as I can be."

The man was in blue overalls, his thin grey hair combed across a well-tanned bald patch. On the table in front of him were a packet of cigarettes, a plastic lighter and a half drunk glass of beer.

Jacques pulled out a chair and sat down. "Gendarme Jacques Forêt," he said, showing the man his identification. "I'd like to ask you a few questions in connection with the disappearance of two tourists." He opened his notebook and placed two photographs on the table. "Just over five weeks ago in May, these two people, who were travelling together, were in this bar and it has been suggested to me that you may also have been here at the same time. Do you recognise either of them?"

155

The man barely looked at the pictures before shaking his head. "It wasn't me," he said and picked up his beer to take a drink. "In May I was on the Limoges to Le Havre run. It can't have been me who was here then."

Jacques sat back his disappointment clearly visible. "You seem very certain about that."

"I am." He gently swilled the remaining amber liquid around the bottom of the glass. "You can check with my employer if you want. This week I'm back on the Limoges to Marseilles run and for the last eight weeks I've been on the north run." He fumbled in the breast pocket of his overalls and pulled out a dog-eared business card. "Logistique Français," he said, scribbling his name and employee number on the back of the card and pushing it across to Jacques. "That's who I drive for and if you ring that number and ask for Sylvie she will tell you whatever you need to know. But it wasn't me." He downed the last of his drink.

"OK. Thanks, but just a couple more questions, Monsieur." He smoothed out the photos of Ekstrom and Anderson. "Can you look closely at the photos and tell me if you have ever seen these people before?" The man shook his head. "And what about these?" Jacques laid out the photos of Kellermann, Myers and Lavoie.

"Sorry," he said as he beckoned the barman. "I don't recognise any of these people except from the papers. They're missing, right?"

"Yes, that's right. Do you ever pick up hitch-hikers?"

"No. It's against company policy and it could cost me my job." The man looked Jacques straight in the eye and then shrugged. "Sorry."

***

Beth watched her hand stirring the lemon tea, swirling the yellow chunk of fruit round and round in the mug and then stabbing it down to the bottom. The steam from the cooling liquid was beginning to abate as a sudden and irrepressible anger made her stop and hurl the spoon across the kitchen and hit the window with such force that a small striated fracture appeared and crept towards one edge of the panel.

"Why?" she bellowed at the ceiling. "Why could you not be honest with me?" Her tears began afresh. Snivelling, she took her tea out into the main living area and looked around. "Which room, Dan? Which?" Then she burst into the master bedroom. Drawers and cupboards open, she began pulling the contents out and throwing them to wherever they landed until she ran out of energy and sank onto the floor light-headed and dizzy.

The tea had toppled over on the dressing table and spilled onto the white fleecy rug beneath, the last few droplets dripping steadily, to add to the pool below. When she surveyed the mess of clothing she recognised that every single item was her own and had come with her from home. She tried to stand but the dizziness returned. "And that's what happens when you stupidly don't eat all day, Beth."

She pushed back her hair and took a deep breath before getting to her feet and steadying herself, and then she crossed the room to right the empty mug.

***

"Anything?" Clergue looked very comfortable behind Jacques' desk as he acknowledged his colleague's return.

"Not really." Jacques let himself in behind the counter and hung up his jacket. "The man at the Drap d'Or wasn't our witness. He's a truck driver and he wasn't even in the area when Ekstrom and Anderson were here. And I cross-checked that by phone with his employer before I left Mende."

"So where does that leave us now, Jacques?"

"For the Swedes, unfortunately, it's another dead end." Jacques dropped his notebook on the desk behind the monitor and looked round to the photos on his notice board. "Yesterday, although Madame Pamier confirmed their arrival here in 2007, she was very tight-lipped about everything else and stated she didn't recognise either the Swedes or Lavoie. She gave absolutely nothing away. When she saw De Silva's photo, her reaction changed. And having considered what she did say, I now think that she was deliberately careful about her answers. At no time did she say where she had lived immediately before coming here. So I want to make some more background checks and then go back and question her more closely." He turned back to Clergue and leaned against the wall. "Anything from England about Samuels?"

Clergue shook his head. "But this has come for Madame Samuels," he said, taking a small padded envelope from off the windowsill at his back. "It was hand-delivered by a woman and she didn't give a name and I haven't had chance to take it round there yet." He handed the package to Jacques.

"But Beth doesn't know anyone here, apart from Marianne and the other women in the village." He turned the envelope over and looked at the back. "There's no sender's name noted," he said.

"Yes, and I did ask for her name but she just said that Beth would know who she was and left in a hurry."

"And that's all?" Jacques stared at his colleague until he squirmed out of his chair and stood.

"She said she was just passing by on her way to St Etienne and didn't have time to go to the chalet and wanted to leave this here for safe-keeping until it could be handed to Beth." He shrugged. "She seemed genuinely concerned, Jacques. I don't see any crime in that." He flopped back into the chair.

"No, you're right, Thibault. Sorry. I'll take this across to her later. By the way, anything from ballistics yet?"

Clergue shook his head and logged out of the computer. "Pelletier called, though. The similarities between our cases and those in the Vercors and Ariège are 'too close for comfort'. His description, not mine."

Jacques nodded. "So we need to start making

connections and quickly. OK." He checked his watch. "It's almost six. I would expect Beth would be back from wherever she's been today, so I'll take this round and then do some more evidence checking. Until tomorrow." He collected his jacket and strode out of the open door.

"You're a very messy packer," said Jacques. He grinned as he leant against the doorjamb and gazed around the disarrayed room.

Beth sat on the bed and looked at him. "I'm not packing," she said flatly. "I'm..." She scooped a pile of clothes off the floor and cradled them on her knee. "I'm not sure what I'm doing."

She stared at the mess. Standing up, she picked up the empty mug.

"I need someone to talk to, Jacques." She stepped past him and, closing the door on the disorganisation, led the way through to the kitchen and dumped the mug in the sink. "That's rage." She pointed at the fractured windowpane as tears began to roll down her cheeks. "Absolute rage."

And then she felt Jacques' arms around her and she let herself sink into the warmth of his body, her cheek pressed against his chest, the rhythmic thud of his heart pulsing beneath his shirt.

"You can talk to me," he said and lightly kissed the top of her head. "You can always talk to me."

"You always make me feel so calm, Jacques," she whispered into his shirt. "No matter what is happening to me you always make me feel calm. How do you do that?"

She felt his gentle touch, his warm breath, as he stroked her hair back over her shoulders.

"I don't know, but I'm glad that I do. Are you going to tell me what this is all about?"

saturday

"Thibault, get me anything we've got on the Devereux," Jacques commanded before his colleague had even taken off his jacket. "The woman who was here yesterday with the package for Beth was Veronique Devereux."

"The Marseille Devereuxes?" Clergue slung his jacket across the counter. "What have they got to do with our investigation?"

"I don't know yet, but Dan Samuels knew Veronique Devereux…" He paused a moment to consider his choice of words. He wanted to shout out loud what he thought of Samuels, but for Beth's sake he said the minimum required. "He knew her quite well, it seems, and my hunch is that the hand gun we found belongs to one of her brothers." He looked back at his computer screen and the pop-up telling him a message had arrived in his in-box from Scotland Yard. He clicked through to his emails. "And that package she left," he looked over the monitor and grinned, "it contained a set of keys to the chalet."

Clergue smiled. "Including a key for the gun cupboard?"

Jacques held up an evidence bag and handed it across the desk. "Front and back doors, garage and gun cupboard," he said. "Can you also chase up those outstanding reports, please, and we need to collect the printouts of the electoral registers from Mende. They are waiting for us."

Clergue nodded and collected his jacket. "OK I'll be back in 45 minutes," he said.

Looking back at his monitor, Jacques began working his way through the various pages of information from the British police.

"Madame Sithrez, what a surprise," said Beth holding the front door open for her visitor to come in with one hand, and holding up a piece of half-eaten toast in the other.

"I've brought you this." She offered Beth the file of proofs. "I've made notes on the back of each of the shots," she said smiling but maintaining her position on the porch. "Have you tried the bramble jam yet?"

Beth blushed as she shook her head. "Not yet. I thought I would follow your advice and wait for a slow morning, which I think might be tomorrow."

"I hope you like it and do let me know if you want any more." Madame Sithrez smiled, then turned and left.

Beth tossed the file onto the bottom step of the spiral staircase as she walked back to the kitchen and the remainder of her breakfast. Before refilling her coffee she opened the fridge and took out the pot of jam and removed the cover. The strong smell of very ripe and sour hedgerow berries filled the air and she breathed in the aroma. She hesitated and then changed her mind and returned the jam to the fridge. Slowly, she closed the door, an impish grin on her face. *I'll have that with some fresh bread tomorrow.* Her coffee replenished, she went up to the loft to finalise her work on the photos.

***

Guy Delacroix hesitated for a moment before he walked into the gendarmerie. Head bowed, he shuffled across to the counter, fished out the receipt for his car tax and pushed it towards Clergue to examine.

"It's done," he said, staring past the policeman. Not listening to the warning he was being given, the farmer remained motionless as he gazed at the numerous photos on Jacques' notice board.

Jacques looked up from his work and followed Guy's line of sight. "What is it, Guy?" He looked at the row of photographs. "What are you looking at?"

Delacroix shrugged and snatched his receipt back, but his attention was again drawn to the photos.

"Do you recognise someone, Guy?" Jacques' tone was becoming more insistent.

"I don't know. Maybe." He turned to leave.

"Hold it right there, Delacroix." Jacques was out from behind the counter in a second and stood between the farmer and the open door of the gendarmerie. "If there's something you want to tell me then do it," he said. "Now," he insisted, strengthening his pose with his hands resting on either side of his belt.

"I'm really not sure," said Delacroix, attempting to move forward.

"Which photo is it that you think you recognise?" asked Clergue as he moved back to give a better view of the board on the opposite wall. "I think you do recognise one of them, don't you?"

Delacroix nodded and edged back to the counter. "The girl," he said. "She's very pretty."

Jacques nodded in agreement. "Yes, she is, but she's missing, Guy, and we have no trace of her or any leads to follow. So, if you know something, tell us now because it could mean the difference between life or death for her." He waited for a response whilst he considered how else he could persuade the old man to talk.

"She just looked familiar, Jacques, that's all." Delacroix shrugged again and turned to leave, but Jacques edged closer.

"OK. That's progress, Guy. Now why is she familiar? Where have you seen her before?" An idea passed through his mind as he looked at how Delacroix was dressed. "Could you have seen her here in the village, or in Mende perhaps?" Recalling the description of the man in the bar, he now realised that Delacroix could have been there at the same time as Ekstrom and Anderson.

Delacroix shook his head and grimaced.

Jacques tried a different tack. "Do you remember the

week of bad weather we had back in May?"

"Of course," he said gruffly. "I had the cattle in the byre for forty-eight hours because of the overnight snow up on the col."

"The girl was in this area then, Guy. Think carefully and tell me what you remember."

"Mende," he said, after a moment. "I went into Mende one day that week." He shuffled his feet and shoved his hands into his pockets. "I went to the Drap d'Or to get out of the rain and I think she was there then."

"With him?" Clergue strode back to the notice board and pointed to the photo of Anderson.

"Yes, I think so." Delacroix peered the second picture. "But I'm not sure."

"Did you see them again after that?" Jacques leaned on the counter and watched the farmer closely.

"The next day, I think. They were at the Sithrez'."

Jacques exchanged a look with Clergue. "Are you sure about that?"

Delacroix stared at the photos again. "Yes, I'm sure," he said, looking from one gendarme to the other. "It was her hair that drew my attention. It was so bright and yellow in the sunshine."

Clergue frowned. "Just a moment," he said rubbing his fingers across his forehead. "Your farm is below the Sithrez and separated by the top road. Their farmhouse is set back off the road by about twenty metres, so, looking up from your property how could you have possibly seen them?"

"I was fixing the roof," he said. "The wind and the rain had dislodged some decaying brickwork and the roof was leaking. It was the first day we had some dry weather that week and I was fixing the roof."

"Show me," said Jacques, nodding to Clergue to come with him as he went back behind the counter to retrieve his jacket and office keys.

As usual, Delacroix's farmhouse was cluttered and scruffy, with an unkempt odour. They followed him up the stairs into the roof space. Jacques had to bend slightly to duck the wooden beams supporting the tiles. At the northerly apex of the roof was a large piece of old sacking that had been inexpertly tacked and taped from the beams to the end wall.

"I was here," said Delacroix, "making this watertight." He pulled at the bottom corner of the sacking and it came away easily.

Jacques stepped forward and squatted down to peer underneath. The brickwork and mortar beneath were crumbling and damp and covered in black mould. He pulled at the sacking and standing upright in the centre of the apex, the only place where he could stand at full height, he wrenched the sacking from the roof support to reveal a hole in the wall about two bricks wide. Through that, he could see the top road and the front door of the Sithrez' farmhouse. Moving aside, he gestured to Clergue to look.

"So you were repairing this," he said as he stepped away and stooped. "Tell me exactly what you did?" He pulled his notebook out of his pocket.

Delacroix sighed. "I had to get the old milking stool from the kitchen to reach the joist," he said. "When I came back up here I saw the girl on the top road walking towards the Sithrez' place."

"Alone?"

"No, with a man. The one in your photo, I think, but I'm not sure." Delacroix shoved his hands in the pockets of his overalls.

"And then?"

"Jean-Arnaud was gardening and he stopped to talk to them as they passed. And then they all went inside."

"Did you see them again that day?"

Delacroix shook his head. "I just got on with my job and that was it."

"Can you remember what time of day this was?"

"Late morning, maybe eleven or a little later. When I finished I went downstairs and got myself something to eat," he said.

Clergue had reattached the sacking as best he could and

was leaning against the wall, listening. "We'll need a statement, Guy," he said.

***

The work for the Sithrez complete apart from the printing, which she would get done in Mende, Beth sat back and rubbed the back of her neck. She stretched her arms above her head and let out a long, low groan. The view across the valley captured her attention and her mind wandered back to yesterday and the meeting in the Notaire's office. Her anger and jealousy resurfaced. She wanted to shout, to scream at Dan for his lack of honesty. But she couldn't. He wasn't there. Then she wondered if he had ever really been there, if he had ever really been with her and, she finally and openly admitted to herself that he probably hadn't. Especially during those last seven years. He'd known about the boy then and, she reasoned, that the knowledge must have coloured his attitudes and arguments, consciously or sub-consciously, whenever she had brought up the subject of children. It was then that she realised that she was the one who always mentioned children. She always instigated those conversations, not Dan. *And now I know why.*

Her eyes were beginning to water, so she distracted herself by loading the shots from St Nicholas onto her laptop and sorting through them. She had some vague idea about creating a set of images to be used for sympathy cards and then quickly revised it and decided that they would just be blank cards for personal messages.

She divided the shots into different folders, inside and outside, statuary and headstones and just allocated each image to its appropriate folder. As the folder labelled 'Headstones' was at the top of the list on the drop-down menu she began there and opened the first image of a black granite headstone. She cropped the photo so that the headstone became the image. She then copied and superimposed it on to another image that contained a background of flowers and plants that she had created from some of the photos she had taken at the Sithrez'. Then she zoomed in on the headstone itself and deleted the names and then re-positioned the short verse in the centre. Zooming in again she went to work on the detail, refining colour shades, sharpening the edges of some of the petals and leaves and finally moving bits and pieces of the background plants and flowers forward so that they looked as though they had purposely grown around the stone. Satisfied with the final version, she saved it.

The next photo was a tall family headstone in red granite that she remembered taking hurriedly but couldn't recall why she had done so. Certain that there would be something useful there, she zoomed in on the text and started reading, first a short verse and then the names. She stopped and stared at the monitor, puzzled.

"How odd," she said. Zooming in further, she peered at the screen to make sure she had not misread the information. "But that means they're more than..." She grabbed a pen and piece of paper and quickly wrote out the calculation. "That's a hundred and twenty-four years ago."

She was still not absolutely certain of the significance of her discovery. Getting a clean piece of paper, she copied the details from the headstone exactly.

***

"Junior Gendarme Mancelle reporting for duty, sir." Pierre ran in through the open door and slid to a halt beside Jacques' desk.

"Hello Pierre, and does your maman know you are here?" Jacques pushed his chair back and scraped it along the wall. When he glanced at Clergue he saw that he had stopped work too.

"No, she thinks I'm playing with Alain and Thierry, but they've gone into the woods and Maman says I can't go there."

"Well, we will have to find some proper police work for

you to do then, Junior Gendarme Mancelle," said Jacques and rose. "And I think I have just the thing." He walked over to the pile of printouts on the counter. "This is a great big list of people," he said.

Pierre's eyes widened. "Bad people?"

Jacques grinned. "No, just ordinary people but we must find the bad people who are hiding in the list, so we need you to help us to put this printout into sets of ten pages each. Can you do that?"

Pierre nodded and Jacques shepherded the boy to the small space behind the counter where he could work on the floor. Then he phoned Marie Mancelle to let her know that her son was safe and with him.

***

"The supermarket was busy again today," said John as he walked through the back door of Ferme Sithrez and placed the bags on the table in front of his wife. "And it's getting hotter," he added as an afterthought.

"Luckily we have the shade on the patio," said Clair as she watched her husband go through the usual routine of setting out the produce for her to check. Checking the first few items, she handed them to John to put in the pantry. "I think Beth has done a wonderful job on those pictures for us, darling, don't you?"

"Yes," came a muffled response from behind the pantry door. "I liked them all," he said re-emerging into the kitchen and collecting some bags of vegetables and retracing his steps. "I like Beth. She's a lovely young woman." He moved jars about on the shelf in the pantry and then counted them.

"She is, darling, isn't she?" Aware that John was taking his time she stopped what she was doing and turned to see that the pantry door was pushed too. "Darling?"

"The jam," said John rushing back into the kitchen. "One of the jars of jam is missing. One of the ones on the right-hand shelf." His face was full of concern.

167

"Yes, I know, darling. We gave it to Beth. Don't you remember? When we took tea to her house, I gave it to her then."

John frowned and hesitated. "No... no," he said, shaking his head. "That was one of the jars from the left-hand shelf, wasn't it? It should have been the left-hand shelf."

"And I'm sure it was, darling. Don't worry. It's just a jar of jam and I can make some more." She smiled at him. "I tell you what, darling. I'll finish putting the shopping away and you put the kettle on and we'll have some tea."

Still a little dazed, John nodded and did as he was asked.

***

"This is a hive of activity," said Beth as she breezed into the gendarmerie and walked straight through the open counter entrance to Jacques' desk. "And I think I've got something from St Nicholas that might be important. Look at...oh!" She noticed Pierre busily ripping sheets of printout apart and then carefully placing them in piles on the floor. "I think this is child exploitation, isn't it?" She grinned at the two men.

Jacques took the piece of paper she held out and read the notes, then passed it to Clergue. "Where has this information come from?"

"A gravestone in the church yard in St Nicholas," she said. "I took some shots whilst I was there and I didn't even know what the inscription said until I started to manipulate the photo." She frowned. "This means their identities are stolen, doesn't it?"

"It's possible, but we need to check and make certain first, Beth. And you can help us with that."

Beth nodded. "Anything. Tell me what to do and I'll do it."

Jacques grinned at her eagerness. "We've got another Jean-Paul here," he said to Clergue and Pierre. "Everyone wants to be a gendarme today. OK. Those births and deaths need to be cross-checked with the records held in the

Archives Départementales in Foix—"

"Oh no. That's another four hour drive there and back, Jacques." Beth pulled a face at the thought.

"You're the one who wants to be a gendarme." He grinned. "This is what police work is all about. The archives are only open on weekdays so you will have to wait until Monday but as they are historical records anyone can consult them."

He turned to Clergue. "You and I need to get on with the research to see if we can get any connections that may be useful to Beth on Monday."

"Can't I help with that?" Beth looked from one to other. "If I've got to wait until Monday I may as well do something useful," she said. "And I still haven't been given permission by the Magistrate to go home yet."

Clergue was about to speak but Jacques jumped in. "We're still waiting for the reports on the handgun we found," he said, watching his colleague closely and hoping that he wouldn't contradict him in the lie. "It could be another week before we can agree to let you leave."

"Let me be useful, then," she said.

"OK. Perhaps you and Junior Gendarme Mancelle can work together in the interview room?"

And in an instant Pierre was on his feet and moving his piles of paper.

"So, we've got that printout done and labelled and in sections of ten pages," said Beth, straightening the large pile in front of her. "You start ripping the next one apart and I'll see what else we need to do."

Pierre nodded but looked at her hard, as though debating whether to ask a question or not. "Why did you break Gendarme Forêt's heart?" His stare was replaced with a deep frown.

Beth looked at the boy, incredulous. "Umm…I didn't know that I had," she said quietly, her cheeks beginning to burn.

"It's what Papa says to Maman when she's cross with

him."

"I see." She took a moment to think how to respond. "Well, I'll just…umm…take these to Jacques," she said and slipped out of the room and the difficult conversation.

To her acute embarrassment she realised that both Clergue and Jacques had heard what Pierre had said. When Jacques smiled at her, the colour in her cheeks deepened.

He looked at his watch and took control. "OK Pierre, it's time for you to go home. Your maman will be cross with me if I keep you here for too long."

The boy presented himself at Jacques' desk and saluted. "Let's go," Jacques said as he and led the way out. As he passed Beth, he whispered, "Can we talk later?"

She nodded.

***

"I don't really know if I should say this, Jacques, but I'm going to anyway," said Clergue as he handed Jacques a mug of coffee later that afternoon. "Letting Beth believe that she is still required here, even when Pelletier has said she is free to go isn't fair." He leaned against the counter and sipped his coffee.

"I just need more time, Thibault."

"So get more time honestly, then."

Jacques looked him straight in the eye. It was the word 'honestly' that brought him up short and he thought back to Friday and how upset Beth had been on finding out about her husbands' son. Honesty had been a word that had been liberally used that evening and now he was using a dishonest approach in the hope of winning her trust. He shook his head as he reproached himself for his stupidity.

"She's worth the trouble, Jacques, if that's what you really want?" Clergue strolled back to his cramped workspace and sat down.

Jacques nodded. "You're right. I'll fix it tonight after work."

Bruno Pelletier removed his spectacles and began polishing the lenses as he considered what Jacques had just told him. "So, Samuels was implicated in a number of cases for fraud and trafficking over a period of five years," he said, summarising the lengthy verbal report he'd just been given.

"But he was never charged," added Jacques. "Only his business manager was charged and convicted."

Pelletier looked up from his mundane task. "Ah. Is that because there really was no evidence or because the business manager was the fall guy?"

"From my reading of the papers and the case notes, there was no real evidence. The detective handling the case emailed me to say that he had had some unanswered questions and that there were times under interview that he felt in his gut that Samuels was not exactly lying but also not exactly telling the absolute truth."

"So," Pelletier replaced his spectacles, "we have, potentially, a very slippery fish here, which brings me to the handgun." He looked over to Clergue.

"No fingerprints found, not even a partial, so it has been thoroughly wiped. The gun hasn't been used for some time but there is an open case and we are waiting to see if there is a match." Clergue referred to his notes. "A naked torso found on a marsh near Marseille, October 2007, fatal gunshot wound to the chest. The other parts of the body, head, arms and legs, have still not been found. Identity of the victim still not known as there were no scars or tattoos from which a positive identification could be made. But a search of missing persons' lists at the time has thrown up a number of possibilities and three of those have connections with the Devereux." Clergue flipped his notebook shut.

"And we now know that Veronique Devereux had a set of keys to the Samuels' chalet." Pelletier reached over to the window and shoved it further open. "This may be a long-shot, but have we cross-checked those three names with your detective at Scotland Yard?"

Jacques grinned. "Already emailed them the names, sir,"

he said.

Pelletier grinned back. "See, Jacques, I knew you were wasted here," he said, thumping the edge of his desk. "OK, the disappearances then, where are we with that work?"

"We now have new information that places Ekstrom and Anderson at Ferme Sithrez just before lunch on the Saturday. A statement has already been taken, but the witness is unreliable. He is a known petty criminal and a drinker, and he has a string of convictions for minor offences," said Jacques.

"We've already interviewed the Sithrez about the Swedish couple and they were both adamant at the time that they had not seen them," added Clergue.

"Interview them again," said Bruno. "But I want to be there when you do."

"We've also come across two connections with St Nicholas and the disappearances there a few years ago. Juan De Silva was known to the Pamiers and he worked for them before they arrived here. The rumour in St Nicholas is that he followed them here, but the Spanish police still have an open case arising from his failure to return to his family in a village in central Spain in November 2007. We are also following up on some information that may show that the Sithrez are using false names but we cannot be sure about that until we check the archives in Foix and cross check for information supplied for Cartes D'Identité."

"Good work," said Pelletier. "Anything else?"

"Three more supposed sightings of Rob Myers have not provided any more leads and the Kellermann case is as it was," concluded Jacques.

The Magistrate fished out some stapled sheets of paper from his drawer. "A list of all the names connected with the disappearances in Ariège and the Vercors." He handed it across the desk to Jacques. "You'll need it for the next stage of the work."

***

"I wasn't expecting to see you again today," said Beth as she strolled down the lane towards her chalet. "Have you been perched on my fence for long?"

Jacques didn't respond as she had expected he would but just stood when she approached.

"And what's the long face for?"

"Let's go inside," he said and held the gate open for her.

"This looks serious." She slotted her key in the lock.

In the cool of the kitchen she poured them both a glass of wine. "So what's this all about?"

Jacques pulled out a stool and sat down. "I need to tell you something," he said. "You are free to leave. The reports we were waiting for have come back and you are not implicated."

"But I thought..." She frowned at him, trying to understand.

"Yes, earlier I said we didn't have them and that wasn't true. I just didn't want you to leave and I stupidly latched on to the first possible opportunity to keep you here." He hesitated and looked at her. "And I'm sorry. I'm really sorry for doing that, Beth."

She took a deep breath. "Well, you could have been honest with me, that's true." She fingered her glass and although she was smarting, she wasn't as angry with him as she thought she should be. Perhaps she had become numb to being treated in this way, she reasoned. But then it hadn't been Jacques who had been dishonest until now, she admitted to herself. "There's been so much dishonesty over these last few weeks, Jacques, that I think I should be really angry with you. But I'm not, I'm just bitterly disappointed."

"And I don't think that that will even come close to how disappointed I am with myself," he said. "It's been eating away at me all day."

She looked at him, the beginnings of smile on her face. "At least that's good. You didn't set out the continue to deceive me for months or years just like..." She glanced out of the window. "Well, you know..."

He nodded and there was a moment of complete

understanding between them.

It was Jacques who broke the temporary silence. "I also need to ask you some more questions about Dan," he said. "And I'm very much afraid that this might mean even more distress for you."

Beth sat upright and took a slug of wine. "I really don't think there can be much more that can surprise me or hurt me, so just say it, Jacques."

"It seems that a few years ago, Dan was involved with someone who was convicted for trafficking and fraud, numerous offences that occurred over a five-year period."

Beth grimaced. "Dan's previous business manager," she said. "Yes, I do know about that. One of the few things he did actually tell me." She let out an ironic laugh. "Can you believe it?" She turned to him and saw the serious look on his face. "But there's more, isn't there?" She downed the remains of her wine and waited.

"It's possible, and this needs to be thoroughly checked first," he said, emphasising the last phrase, "that there is a connection to the Devereux in Marseille. A known family of criminals who dabble in people and drugs trafficking."

Beth stared at him and then carefully placed her glass on the breakfast bar. "That last bit I definitely didn't know. When Dan told me the problems his businesses were having, he said it was because his then business manager was making withdrawals without permission, moving money around without consultation and making investments that Dan hadn't approved. The work to renovate the cottages in Northumberland arose apparently because the business manager had let the properties to some unsavoury individuals who then trashed both places." She stopped and thought for a moment. "At least, that's what he told me at the time."

"It was drugs, Beth. Those properties were being used as drugs farms according to the British Police. So for Dan to say the properties were trashed by the occupants would have actually been true. To put the interiors right, he would have had to gut them."

Beth frowned. "Well, thank you for trying to make it sound better than it is but even you cannot change the basic fact that Dan lied to me for most of our time together."

sunday, october 22nd, 1968

"Mr Matherson?" The policeman removed his hat and repeated his question. "Mr John Matherson?"

Stunned and silent, John looked from the male officer to the shorter female constable and back again. "Yes, but I don't understand…"

"Can we come in, Mr Matherson, if you don't mind," asked the young woman.

"Yes." He held the door open and stepped aside. "Just through there," he said, pointing to a solid wooden door to the right. "Mother, it's the police," he shouted as he closed the front door and followed after them into the main room.

The two officers stood together and when asked to sit down did so.

"I'm Sergeant Sam McKinley and this is my colleague, Constable Jane Winters, and I'm afraid we have a serious matter to discuss with you, Mr Matherson.

John glanced at his mother and then the constables. "It's Annie, isn't it? It's my little Annie?" Tears were beginning to glisten in his eyes.

"We don't know that yet, sir, but can you tell me where your daughter is at the moment?"

John sniffed loudly. "Yes, it's Sunday and she always goes round to her friend Amy's house on a Sunday, for her tea. It gives my mother a bit of a rest from looking after her whilst I'm out at work all week."

"So there's no Mrs Matherson, then?" The WPC thought again. "I mean, does Annie's mum not still live with you here?"

John shook his head. "Walked out when Annie was just three. Don't know where she is and don't want to."

176

"And when would you be expecting Annie back from her friend's house?"

John looked at the clock and noticed it was almost five-thirty. "About now," he said. "Anytime now. She's always on time, you know."

"And can you tell me what your daughter was wearing today, Mr Matherson?"

"Something's happened. Where is she? Why won't you tell me what's happened?" His distress was beginning to get the better of his already strained composure.

"We know how difficult this must seem, Mr Matherson, but we have to be sure," said McKinley. "Can you tell me what clothes your daughter had on today?"

John looked over to his mother who was huddled by the blazing coal fire.

"It were her blue dress and coat, John, and her white cardigan," the old lady said quietly as she stretched out her hand to place it on her son's forearm for comfort.

The constables exchanged a look and McKinley gave a slight nod to his colleague.

"I'm really sorry to have to tell you that there's been an accident, and we believe that your daughter may be involved and I'm going to have to ask you…"

John Matherson stopped listening as his shoulders convulsed under the weight of the constrained sobs and tears that began to course down his face.

sunday, june 2009

Beth's drive to Foix had been pleasant and unhurried, unlike her visit to St Nicholas. To give herself plenty of time for her research at the archives, she had booked a room overnight in the town centre with the option of a second night if required. Her room overlooked the central square, which was bathed in warm sunlight, the gentle breeze rustling through the canopies of the plane trees. She'd travelled light and in less than ten minutes had unpacked and was looking out of her open window across the square.

The room was functional, but tastefully decorated and contained only the essential furniture: bed, desk, TV, minibar and integral bathroom. She turned away from the window and stared at the picnic hamper that she'd placed on the desk, alongside her laptop, and wondered what was in there. A smile crossed her face as she thought about how insistent Jacques had been that she should have a picnic to take with her.

"Well, that's dinner sorted for tonight," she said to herself and then realised that her only other alternative would have been to eat alone in the hotel restaurant. She screwed her nose up at the idea and fished her phone out of her handbag and dialled.

"I'm here," she said. "And thank you again for the hamper. I still haven't opened it yet. I think I will have a walk around and if I can find a park close by then I will take it with me and eat there."

And then she listened as Jacques pointed out to her that Foix was a much larger place than Messandrierre and a park on a Sunday evening may not be the right place for someone alone who is not local.

"Always the policeman, Jacques," she said, trying her best to sound like a scold. "Always the policeman."

She ended the call.

monday

"…and the targets on car checks are down," said Fournier, "with the holiday season no more than a couple of weeks away we need to actively work on that."

"Yes, sir." Jacques quietly and carefully dropped the envelope containing his resignation onto the back of Fournier's desk.

Fournier looked up for a second. "I know Clergue has been working out at Messandrierre on a regular basis recently but Magistrate Pelletier needs him here in Mende. So I've told him to report here from tomorrow."

"Yes, sir," said Jacques as he tried to confine a smirk.

"When this missing persons' enquiry is concluded, I will be reviewing the allocation of resources, and I want to forewarn you that I will most likely be assigning you to our central team here in Mende," he said. "But nothing is final."

Jacques wasn't going to say anything at first but then realised that in view of the content of the letter he had just delivered it might be politic to play along.

"Well, if nothing is final can I please let you know that my preference would be to stay in Messandrierre, sir?"

Fournier looked up and studied his face. "You're wasted there. I can find work here for you that is much better suited to your talents." His attention was again focussed on his papers. "Next week at ten," he said.

As Jacques closed the door on Fournier's office he wondered if he had really heard what had just been said. *Has Fournier just acknowledged that I'm a better cop than he will ever be?* He shook his head to rid himself of what he knew to be an utterly ridiculous thought.

"That man's a robot," he said to himself as he put his

helmet on and started the bike. Then he considered the fleeting conversation for a moment and wondered if Pelletier might have said something on his behalf. A grin on his face he sped back to his office and his work.

***

Ploughing through the indexes and lists of births and deaths was a more tedious task than Beth had ever thought possible, but her perseverance had paid off as she waited for Jacques to answer his phone.

"It all checks out," she said when he finally did. "Jean-Arnaud, born December 21ˢᵗ 1885, parents Beatrice and Bertrand. Born in St Nicholas and died February 18ᵗʰ 1886 of consumption."

She waited for him to make his notes before continuing. "His older sister, Esclairmonde, born April 4ᵗʰ 1883, parents also Beatrice and Bertrand and she died of consumption on February 28ᵗʰ 1886."

Beth put her phone away and then ordered copies of entries in the registers. An hour later she was driving through Foix on her way back to Messandrierre.

***

"What the hell is the meaning of this?" shouted Fournier as he stood and waved Jacques' letter in his face. It was 4 p.m. and Jacques was back in Mende following a summons.

"I think it is quite self-explanatory," he said, not shifting his ground and determined to keep his cool.

"You know exactly what I'm asking you," Fournier said, his tone threatening. "I don't have to accept it, you know," he continued when no answer was forthcoming. "I can refuse your resignation if I choose."

Jacques thought about all the notes he had made and kept about his dealings with Fournier and all the information he'd amassed where the work could have been handled more efficiently and effectively and smiled inwardly. "Yes, you can, sir, if you want a fight on your hands and the HR department all over your command, sir."

Fournier glared at him, barely able to contain his rage. "So, this is just about revenge, is it? Because you think you are the better policeman," he sneered as he paced backwards and forwards behind his desk.

"No, sir. This is a carefully planned change of career path for me and I would be grateful if you would accede to my request." Jacques remained standing, his hands crossed behind his back.

"Change of career path!" Fournier bellowed. "Back to Paris, is it? Back to the Judiciaire?" He leaned forward on his desk.

Jacques wanted to tell him to mind his own business but thought better of it. "No, sir. As much as I enjoy work in investigation I have no wish to live in Paris again and I think I will be staying here in Mende." And before Fournier could remind him where the door was Jacques was in the corridor and running to the yard for his bike.

In Pelletier's office, Clergue was halfway through an update for the Magistrate on the day's findings when Jacques walked in.

"...the information from the archives in Foix suggests that Monsieur and Madame Sithrez are using assumed names and we are awaiting the results of further checks. The Pamiers were implicated in the disappearance of De Silva and another young man who worked for them in St Nicholas and were questioned about all the other disappearances there as well. As yet we cannot link either the Pamiers or the Sithrez to the disappearances in the Vercors."

"But we can't ignore the recent new information about three of the missing persons being seen last by the Sithrez," said Pelletier.

Jacques nodded his agreement.

"Have we got enough for a warrant to search both their properties?" asked Clergue.

The Magistrate thought for a moment. "Not really, but

there is no reason why we cannot anticipate a search of both their properties and get the paperwork started on the basis that we will confirm the need as soon as," he said. "And we still need to question the Pamiers about whether De Silva really did follow them here."

"Madame Pamier, do you recognise this man?" Jacques placed the photo of Juan De Silva on the kitchen table in front of her.

She looked down and nodded, her thin lips pressed tightly together.

"How do you know him, Madame?"

"He worked for us in St Nicholas. He used to help me on the farm and with the animals." Her face was weathered and she looked older than her years, but in her expression there was nothing for Jacques to read.

"Did he work for you full-time or was there some other arrangement?"

"He worked for us only when he was in the village. He moved around a lot." She sat very still and stared at Jacques as he jotted her answer down in his notebook.

"Juan De Silva was reported missing in November 2007, Madame, and he still has not been found. When did you last see him?"

"September 2006."

"You seem very sure about that, Madame. It's almost three years ago. Are you sure you don't want to take a little more time to think about that?"

"I don't need more time," she said sharply. "I've already answered questions like this before and I don't have time to waste on answering the same questions again, Gendarme Forêt." She clenched her teeth and glared at him.

Jacques picked up the photo and slotted it into the back of his notebook. "Did Juan ever come and work for you here in Messandrierre?"

"Another question I've answered before. No!" She spat the word at him.

"So you are absolutely certain that you have not seen

Juan De Silva since September 2006. Is that correct?"

"Yes," she said and stood up. "Now if you don't mind, I have work to do."

"So do I, Madame, and I'm not finished yet. So, we can sit here and answer questions or you can come with me to the gendarmerie and answer my questions there. Your choice, Madame."

Madame Pamier hesitated and stared at Jacques, then sat down, her hands clasped and resting on the table in front of her.

"Have you ever lived in the Vercors, Madame?" Jacques watched her closely.

"Yes." She looked down.

"Would you like to tell me where and how long ago that was?" He sat back and studied her face searching for the slightest change.

"St Agnan. I had a small-holding there from 1998 to 2002." She frowned as she thought for a moment. "Yes, it was 2002 when we left."

"And you left to move to St Nicholas, is that correct?"

"Yes."

"Do these names mean anything to you, Madame?" He unfolded a single sheet of paper and placed it in front of her. She barely glanced at the list before answering.

"I know three of them," she said. "Didier Praud, Michel Martin and Francis Rousseau. They all worked for me from time to time." With the flat of her hand, she pushed the piece of paper back towards him. "And I already know that they went missing and I was questioned by the police at the time," she said before Jacques could pose his next question. "It was why we left in the end. All the rumours in the village and the gossip. I couldn't stand it."

Jacques made a note and then checked his notebook for any other outstanding queries. "One last thing, Madame, how well do you know Monsieur and Madame Sithrez?"

She looked at him and frowned. "Not that well," she said. "I keep myself to myself and I mind my own business."

"So you've never come across the Sithrez before they

moved here?"

Madame Pamier just nodded in agreement.

***

"I'm sorry to be later than planned," Jacques said as he followed Beth to the dinner table which was set with a simple salad and a basket of bread. He noted the care that she had taken with everything and pulled out a chair and sat. "I suppose this is for you to tell me that you are going home, isn't it?"

Beth wasn't sure how to answer. She'd spent most of her drive back thinking about Jacques. She'd also revisited the embarrassing moment when Pierre had questioned her more times than she cared to admit. And on each occasion she had found herself blushing in response.

"Yes and no," she said quietly. "I wanted to return your hospitality but I also think we need to talk. You did ask me after the bonfire if we could talk about us and we still haven't done that yet."

"Yes I know," he said, despondent. "But I've taken it that perhaps you are right...and that there is no future for us."

Beth looked at him. This wasn't what she had wanted to hear nor was she expecting it. Yes, she did have to go home; there were things she needed to put in place so that she could come back. The time in the car had helped her to clarify her own thoughts and she had decided to come back, at least for a while. She'd also decided that she would ring the estate agent and take the chalet off the market. It might have been Dan's wish that the place be sold, but the deeds were in her name and she had come to the conclusion that the decision to sell or not was entirely hers. She took a deep breath. "Is that what you really want?"

He looked at her and reached across and stroked her cheek. "No, Beth. It's not what I really want. But if it's not right for you, then I think I have to accept that."

No longer hungry, she pushed her plate away. "I'm not sure what is right for me any more, Jacques. So much has happened these past few days and weeks. And Dan…" she shrugged, "he seems to be shadowing me everywhere I go."

Jacques nodded. "But he's not here and I am," he said, gently covering her hand with his and giving it a squeeze.

"I know," she said. "And I think I like that." She smiled.

tuesday

Clergue was gone and Jacques was back at his desk and had the gendarmerie to himself again. But not for much longer. The thought brought a self-satisfied grin to his face as he glanced through the details in the letter in his hand. Picking up the phone, he dialled the number in Mende and asked for Alain Vaux.

"Jacques Forêt. I received your letter yesterday… Thank you… Yes, a discussion over lunch would be fine. But I need to explain that I am in the middle of an important investigation at the moment so my time is fully committed… In two weeks' time?" He waited for the response. "Thursday the sixteenth will be fine, and thank you."

He scribbled a note on his desk pad as the postman walked in.

"Not much today," said Jean-Paul, leaving three envelopes on the counter. "You look like you've just eaten an enormous bowl of cream."

"I have," said Jacques. "I've resigned my job and I've just arranged a meeting with someone that I hope is going to be my new boss and possibly, in the not too distant future, a business partner."

Jean-Paul was aghast. "Congratulations…but I thought you were settled here, and I never thought you would leave the gendarmerie, Jacques." He placed his large stubby hands on the counter as if to steady himself. "I can't believe it," he said. "I just can't believe it."

"Well, do believe it. In two weeks I will be out of here and working for Vaux Investigations in Mende."

The postman grinned and nodded. "See, I knew you

couldn't leave police work behind," he said. "And to complete the picture all you need now is a good woman!"

Jacques picked up the post and smiled. "And I think I might just do that. Ça va."

He turned back to his desk to begin the tedious job of working through the electoral registers.

***

Beth had spent the early part of the morning in Mende. At the printers', she had collected the completed cards, and later at the stationers', she had found envelopes that would suit. Back at the chalet, she carefully slotted each card under the lip of its own envelope as she wondered about how to charge for her work. The cost of the printing, the card and the envelopes she felt certain should be passed onto John and Clair. But the need to put a value on her time and her artistic flair in creating the finished product was a more difficult problem. She could not begin to imagine how to assign a value on her creativity.

"But this is business," she reminded herself. "And if I want to make this a success, I have to come up with a cost for my work."

With the cards neatly arranged in a box, she covered it with the lid and, running her hand across the midnight blue of the top, she decided that she would need to create a proper invoice. "Hmm, but what do I include in the charge," she wondered. On a scrap of paper she jotted down some notes: cost of box, envelopes, printing, card and time. She looked up and thought about how many hours to charge for and decided on two, even though she knew it was woefully inadequate. She chewed the end of her pencil as the thorny issue of the value of her artistry came to the forefront of her mind again.

"Beth, two years ago you would have just asked Dan and he would have..." Told me not to be so ridiculous and that the money I could earn was not needed, she thought. But it wasn't the money that was the issue, the real issue. It was her need to be useful, to be independent and to be, for once, her own person, alone. Looking at the list again she drew a line through it, turned the page over and began again: materials, professional fee, hours.

***

Pelletier sat opposite Jacques and listened.

"…the Pamiers are shown on the registers in the Vercors and Ariège for the years that we know they were there. The Sithrez are not registered anywhere. We only know that they came from St Nicholas because they have told others in the village that that is so. But there is no trace of them or anyone by that name for the years we're interested in. In addition, I can find no trace of anything for them before 2007. We know they were the last to see Myers, Ekstrom and Anderson and they could fit the description of the couple seen in Mende talking to Kellermann."

"And the Pamiers?" Pelletier sat back in his chair.

"In all three villages at the right time in every instance, but we have no clear evidence of them being seen with or talking to our victims."

Pelletier frowned. "So who are the Sithrez?" He looked at Jacques. "If you believe they are here under a false name, then who are they? And why are they using a false name?"

"I can't answer that yet," he said.

Pelletier stood. "We'll question them further this afternoon at two," he said. "Separately and here," he added.

Jacques nodded and picked up the telephone to make the arrangements.

***

Beth knocked on the open door. "Hello, it's me," she called, and then she heard John coming down the narrow staircase.

"Come in," he said, a bright smile on his face as he held the door to the kitchen open for her.

"I've brought your cards," she said, placing the box on the kitchen table. "And this is my invoice." She handed him a sealed envelope and hoped he wouldn't open it until after she had gone.

"Oh, yes." He took it from her and put it on top of the box. "Clair will deal with that for you."

Beth hesitated for a moment unsure of what to say next. "Well, I'd better be going then. Bye."

And as she turned to go she was aware that John remained exactly where he was and didn't show her out. Odd, she thought, but almost instantly shook the concern from her mind and took the steep path down the hill to call on Jacques.

***

"Just the person I need," Jacques said as she walked in. He got up and walked to her side of the counter. "I need to talk to you about the Sithrez."

"I've just come from there," she said.

Placing his hand gently against the middle of her back, he encouraged her to move forward. "In the interview room, over here."

At the doorway she stopped and looked up at him. "Is this a formal interview, Jacques?"

He smiled and took her hand in his and led her into the room. "No, but I will need to take notes. Sit there and I'll get my notebook."

Back in moment, he sat opposite her, his face composed seriousness.

She smiled at him. "Always the policeman, Jacques, always."

"Only until the end of this investigation," he countered and returned her smile. "The Sithrez," he said, adopting his usual business-like tone. "You found out and confirmed that the names they are using are false. But you've spent quite a bit of time with them and I want you tell me anything that you can remember that might help us."

Beth took a breath and thought for a moment. "I first met John at the supermarket in Montbel. I was chaining up my bike and he spoke to me. I think that was when he said that he and his wife had moved here."

"And what did you think he meant by that?" Jacques put his pen down, sat back and crossed his arms.

"I suppose I took him to mean that he and his wife had moved here permanently from home." She pushed her hair back over her shoulders as she tried to recall the details. "He told me his wife's name then, too, and referred to her as Clair. He didn't tell me his surname though."

"So at that point you wouldn't have known they were French?"

She looked at him, puzzled. "Well, of course I wouldn't have thought that. He spoke to me in perfect English," she said flatly. She frowned again. "And…"

Jacques leaned his elbows on the table. "Go on. This case is baffling enough already, so anything you say, no matter how odd it might seem, is OK," he encouraged her.

"Whenever I've been with them, we've always spoken English except…" She stopped as though reluctant to go on.

"Except?" He waited. "You can tell me anything, Beth." He reached across the table and gently rubbed her arm.

"The night of the fête. Except then. I know I was busy with the photographs and everything and I hardly had chance to speak to them at all. But when one of the other guests on the same table as the Sithrez asked me for a picture I just said 'hello' to them in passing but they both answered in French." She stopped again, looked at him and shrugged. "I don't know what that means but I didn't think anything of it at the time."

Jacques nodded. "OK, and can you think of anything they might have said about their respective pasts?" Trying not to put words into her mouth, he paused. "For instance, might they have mentioned family, perhaps?"

She thought back over all her conversations with them and shook her head. "No, nothing. And thinking about it, you would expect people of their age to have family,

wouldn't you? Grand-children or a son or daughter at least."
She shook her head again and then sighed. "No, I don't
think they have ever mentioned family. In fact they've
hardly ever talked about themselves at all, except in
connection with this village. When I first went there for 'tea
and cakes', as they referred to it, I did think how out of
place her English bone china cups and saucers were in that
old and traditional French farmhouse. And yet it never
occurred to me ask what the connection was, not then, nor
later." She slumped back in her chair. "This isn't helping
you at all, is it?"

"Yes, it is, Beth. Just keep talking to me." He smiled
encouragingly. "What else did you talk about?"

"Photography and the commission they gave me for the
personal Christmas cards. We spent quite a bit of time
debating what the pictures on the cards should look like, so
I only learned what their tastes were. Well, Clair's tastes,
really. I think she is very much in charge in that household."

Jacques grinned. "Marianne thinks the same," he said. A
thought occurred to him and he shifted tack. "Would you be
able to pinpoint where they might have come from or have
lived in England?"

Her face brightened and she nodded. "John has the
remnants of an accent from the north of England or possibly
Newcastle but I can't be more precise than that. Clair is
more difficult. She doesn't seem to have any kind of accent
at all. She just speaks straight, flat, correctly pronounced
English." She shrugged. "Sorry."

"No…this is OK, Beth. It's a start. Anything else?"

She put her hands at either side of her head and rubbed
her fingers backwards and forwards across her brow as she
stared at the table for a minute or so. "Just now," she said
suddenly looking up, "when I took the cards John seemed to
be all by himself in the house and he seemed…agitated, I
suppose."

"I phoned him earlier to invite him here at two to help us
with our enquiries. It was probably nothing more than that,"
he said and stood. "If I get finished here early enough, can I

come round to see you later?"

Beth grinned at him. "I'd like that. Maybe you can try some of my baking. I'm going home now to make some scones to have with the jam Clair gave me," she said, a wide smile on her face as she passed in front of him.

But he couldn't let the moment go and he caught her arm, pulled her close to him and kissed her.

At the open doorway of the gendarmerie Jacques was waiting for the Magistrate to arrive, when he saw the vet's car pull off the RN88 and onto the D6. Jacques waved and Fabian pulled up a few feet away.

"The postman tells me you're moving on," Fabian shouted through his open car window. "Going private, I hear!"

Jacques walked across to him, grinning, "Jean-Paul is the worst gossip in this village."

"So it's not true, then?" Fabian frowned.

"Oh, yes, it's true. It's just that I didn't expect the postman to blab to the whole of his round."

"Congratulations, mate. Got to go, I'm expected at Ferme Rouselle in five. We've got to catch up," he shouted as he set off. "And soon."

Jacques waved him off and strolled back as Pelletier parked up.

"I wanted to be here before they arrived," Pelletier said, as he led the way inside.

"It's Monsieur Sithrez at two, and I haven't made any arrangements for Madame yet. I thought we would see what we could get from him first."

Pelletier nodded and walked through to the interview room and sat down by the wall. "I want you to do the questioning to start with. I will just see where that leads us and then I will gradually start asking supplementary questions until I then have command of the whole interview. Are you happy with that?" Jacques nodded; it was a strategy that he had used himself during his time in Paris and a strategy that he had always found to work well.

Monsieur Sithrez was ten minutes late and, once settled in the interview room, Jacques began quietly by introducing his colleague. He explained that the process was just routine and that they needed help with their enquiries. He eased gently into the questioning.

"Monsieur Sithrez, how long have you lived here in Messandrierre?" He flipped open his notebook ready to take down the answer.

"Since the summer of 2007," said John.

"Have you lived anywhere else in France, Monsieur?" Jacques watched him closely and noted that John looked across at the Magistrate and then back to himself.

"We've travelled all over France," he said. "But we like living here. It's a nice village."

Jacques noted the evasion. "So where else in France have you lived, Monsieur?"

"We've lived all over the country," he said after a moment.

It was just the lead Jacques needed. "Can you tell me the names of some of the places where you've lived?"

John shrugged. "I can't remember them all," he said, half laughing. "There have been too many."

Jacques decided to change tack. He glanced at Pelletier who was stony-faced and clearly intending to remain silent for the moment.

"Can you give me your date of birth, Monsieur? Just for our records." Jacques leant forward.

"Twenty-seventh of May, 1942," he said.

"And where were you born?" As there was no immediate response he added, "just for our records, Monsieur."

"Here," John said simply. He scraped his chair back as far as it would go and leant forward, resting his arms on his thighs, his hands clasped together.

Jacques took a sideways glance at Pelletier and continued. "Here in Messandrierre?"

"Oh, sorry no I meant here in France."

"This is a big country, Monsieur. Can you tell me where exactly?"

"St Nicholas in Ariège," he said.

Jacques noted the details and then flipped back to another page in his notebook. "As I am sure you are aware, Monsieur, it is compulsory to register all births in this country and there is no record of a birth for Jean-Arnaud Sithrez in 1942 in St Nicholas."

John squirmed in his seat but made no attempt to explain or challenge Jacques' statement. As the silence lengthened, John visibly became more uncomfortable. He pulled his watch further down his wrist and then pushed it back up again. He shuffled round in his chair so that only Jacques was in his direct line of sight.

Consulting his notebook again, Jacques continued. "We have a record of a child with your name being born in St Nicholas in 1885 who then died in February the following year. We've checked with the archives in Foix and we've checked for surviving children of that family and there are none. The last surviving son of that family was Bertrand Arnaud Sithrez, born in 1914, unmarried, and who was shot during the Second World War."

He waited for a response but John just stared at the floor. Jacques took a sideways glance at Pelletier.

"Would you like to tell me who you really are, Monsieur?"

John finally looked at the Magistrate. "I had to do it," he said to Pelletier. "I had to do it." He turned to Jacques, a fine mist in his eyes. "She threatened Beth," he said.

Pelletier snatched Jacques' pen and notebook out of his hands. "Go!" He shouted.

Jacques was sprinting up the D6 in seconds. He leapt the gate and raced to the entrance. He took the three steps to the porch in one leap and crashed through the door. Beth was standing but only just. Her left hand against the wall she was desperately gasping for air. Jacques pulled out his mobile and hesitated for a split second. He dialled.

"Fabian, urgent. Bring your search and rescue bag. Beth's chalet. Now!"

He caught Beth just a she was about to hit the floor. He checked her pulse. It was racing. He put her in the recovery position. She was still gasping for breath.

"Come on, Fabian," he shouted and then checked that her airway was clear.

"I'm here," said Fabian as he ran through the open door and slid to his knees next to Beth.

"Pupils hugely dilated, pulse racing, airway clear, respiration laboured," shouted Jacques. He phoned 112 and relayed the details to the control centre.

"Don't watch, Jacques," said Fabian as he made the incision in her neck to enable him to keep her breathing. "We need to moisten her lips. Find some lip salve or something – and hurry."

tuesday, 6.12 p.m.

Search warrant in hand, Pelletier joined Jacques and Clergue at the front door of Ferme Sithrez. "Will Beth pull through?"

"I don't know yet, but she's in the best place and I can't do anything more to help her."

"You don't have to be here for this if you would rather be in Mende with Beth."

Jacques shook his head. "I'd rather be busy and at work than pacing hospital corridors," he said.

Pelletier nodded.

Jacques knocked on the door and waited. When there was no response he knocked again. This time, he tried the door handle and pushed. It wasn't locked. Before entering he called out, "Madame Sithrez. It's Gendarme Forêt, Madame."

Again there was only silence.

Jacques looked back at Pelletier. "You take upstairs, Jacques, and Clergue, you're with me for downstairs and the outbuildings and garden."

Jacques pulled on his gloves and entered slowly.

"Madame Sithrez," he called again and waited. He looked around the hallway to see if there was anything unusual or different, but the coats hung up by the door were just as on his previous visits and the door to the kitchen was closed. He climbed the stairs, consciously looking at each step for anything out of place before he stood on it. At the landing, he stopped and looked around. There was a faint breeze from his left. The door ahead of him was closed, as was the first on his left. The second on the left was ajar. He went towards it, reached forward and slowly pushed the

197

door back. He sniffed and there it was. The unmistakable acrid scent of death barely masked by the fresh air from the open window opposite.

Standing in the doorway, he scanned the room. On his left stood a large oak wardrobe, ahead was a dressing table below the window and, as he moved further forward and looked to his right, he saw the lifeless body on the bed. He looked at the flaccid skin around the neck and the staring eyes and realised that she was much older than he had imagined. Without her large round glasses, her sunken eyes looked pale and weak. Her hair – her real hair – was grey and thin and short and without any form of style. Her wig was on a stand on the small dressing table, the sun accentuating the copper hue as it streamed in through the open window.

"In here," he shouted as he reached across to check for a pulse. It was too late.

Whilst he waited for his colleague to join him, he automatically began a careful search of the room. The wardrobe was full of only her clothes, all arranged neatly and beginning with white on the left and running through the whole colour spectrum to black on the right. Obsessive? Probably, he decided. He checked for anything hidden at the back and in the corners and then turned his attention to the large drawer underneath. In there, neatly laid out and at the back, were numerous mobile phones, the backs beside each one and the sim removed and placed on top of each of the displays. Towards the front of the drawer and in line with each of the phones were various other items. Two watches, a scrunchy and a copper bracelet. On the far right of the drawer was a brown folder. He carefully lifted the top cover to reveal newspaper cuttings, hand-written notes, and various other papers as Pelletier walked into the room.

"It's Madame Sithrez, and there's no pulse. We'll need all this photographed and bagged." He let the cover drop back and closed the drawer.

Pelletier nodded and took out his phone.

A moment or two later Clergue sprinted up the stairs.

"The outhouse," he shouted as he stood on the landing to catch his breath. "You both need to see this. It's Myers."

wednesday, 9.06 a.m.

Jacques hated hospitals with a vengeance. Always white, grey and hot, and he could never understand why they all smelt the same. He looked at his watch and calculated that he'd been on duty for twenty-five hours. *That'll please Fournier and his damned budget!*

The window of the waiting room on Beth's ward looked across the rooftops of Mende and he stood there transfixed. He checked his watch again. That was another thing about hospitals he hated, the endless, pointless waiting. To relieve the boredom and inactivity, he went to the floor below and got himself a plastic cup of vile brown stuff that purported to be coffee from the machine in the stairwell at the opposite end of the building. As he strode back to the waiting room, he prayed for the millionth time that Beth would be OK.

Back in front of the window again, he pulled out his mobile with the intention of calling Pelletier for an update. Staring at the display he changed his mind and switched it off. When he heard the door open, he turned round.

"Gendarme Forêt?"

"Yes." Jacques waited as the doctor came into the room and closed the door.

"Please sit down," he said as he settled himself on the edge of a chair.

"Beth Samuels has had a restful night and if her test results come back clear we should be able to release her later today." The doctor paused to let the information register. "She will need to take things easy for the next few days and it would be a good idea if there was someone with her until she is fully fit again," he said.

Jacques put his coffee on the floor beside his chair and pressed his fingers into his tired eyes. "OK," he said and swallowed hard to dispel the lump in his throat.

"Are there any family members here in France that we need to contact?"

"No. She's here in France alone."

"You look worn out, Gendarme Forêt. I think you should go home, and if you leave me your number we'll ring you if there's any change."

"Yes, I am. I've been on duty for the last 24 hours. Thank you," he said, handing the doctor his card.

"I'm sure she'll make a complete recovery," the doctor said as he left the room.

Dazed but relieved, Jacques remained sitting there for a while longer, the coffee untouched on the floor beside him.

By eleven Jacques was changed and back in Mende in an interview room with Pelletier.

John sat at the other side of the table. He had had some sleep but there were hollow marks under his eyes and his face was ashen and drawn. He sat motionless, staring at the wall behind the Magistrate.

Jacques took his cue from Pelletier and began quietly.

"John, we need you tell us who you are?"

John began rocking backwards and forwards in his seat. "I had to do it," he said. "I had to do it for Beth."

"John? Is that your real name?" He waited but John neither looked at him nor answered his question.

"I had to do it. For Beth. For all of them." He kept on repeating himself until Jacques interrupted him.

"Who, John? Who are you talking about?"

"GosiaKaminskiThaddeusKanesMaryMa...." The series of names that followed became incomprehensible as he laid his head on the table and broke down in uncontrollable tears.

"Monsieur Myers has had a restful night. He is hooked up to a drip and we are monitoring his progress hourly at the moment." The doctor closed a file on his desk. "He is undernourished, has clearly suffered a number of beatings but those remaining injuries will heal fully over the next few days. The injuries to his wrists and ankles will take a little longer."

"Is he fit enough to answer some questions?" Pelletier was keen to move the investigation on.

"Monsieur Myers has suffered some mental trauma, but my colleague is of the opinion that, with the right counselling and treatment, he should make a full recovery, but it will be some time before he does so. So, yes, you can question him but I can only give you an hour and he must not be distressed in any way."

The doctor rose and led Jacques and Pelletier to Rob's room. Opening the door for them, he left them to their work.

Jacques brought a second chair from under the window and placed it beside the bed. Pelletier took the chair on the opposite side and nodded to Jacques to begin.

Rob Myers was thin and his face drawn and grey, and there were numerous cigarette burns on the insides of his arms. He looked from one to the other. "Police?" His voice was quiet and a little hoarse.

"Gendarme Jacques Forêt and Investigating Magistrate Pelletier." Jacques pulled out his notebook. "Can you tell us what happened to you?"

"The plants," he said. "If I hadn't have seen the plants I wouldn't have…I wouldn't have…" He began to quiver as he tried to stop the tears but they came streaming down his face.

Jacques was patient. "Where were you, Rob, when you saw the plants?"

He wiped his face and tried to compose himself. "The chateau. Taking photographs. From the very top you can see over the wall into their garden." He stopped to take a sip of water from the glass on his bedside table. "My mum's a botanist and I recognised some of the plants. As I walked by on the road, John was in his front-garden and I started to talk to him about his garden. He invited me in."

His resolve began to waiver and he drew his thumb and forefingers across his eyes until they pinched the bridge of his nose. "She made me some tea and there were some scones and jam and we talked about the garden. It's full of poisonous plants. There's Monks Head and Belladonna and Foxglove. More. And then I began to feel strange, and the next thing I knew I was on the floor in some sort of cellar, chained to the wall." The colour drained from his already pale face and he began to tremble.

Jacques jumped up and called a nurse.

Outside the room Pelletier was pacing. "My God, who are these people?" he said. "I don't think we can press him for much more at this stage."

"I agree," said Jacques. "But I would like to show him the photos of the other missing persons in our patch. He may recognise someone."

Pelletier stopped and considered this for a moment. "Go ahead," he said and recommenced his pacing.

"You can go in now." The nurse held the door open for them and Jacques and Pelletier resumed their seats.

"Just a couple more questions, Rob, then we'll leave you to rest."

Myers laid his head back on the pillow. "Yes, OK."

"I've got some photos for you to look at and I want you tell me if you recognise any of them?"

Rob nodded.

Jacques held up the pictures one by one starting with Venka Ekstrom.

"Dead. I buried her in the garden. I had no choice. It was either do as she said or…"

Jacques nodded and showed him Leif Anderson's photo next.

"The same."

Rob's response for the photo of Alain Lavoie was as before. Jacques knew it was a long shot but he held up the picture of Dieter Kellermann all the same.

Rob shook his head. "No, I don't know who that is."

"OK. Thanks, Rob. Can you tell me where to find these

graves?"

"The top two flower beds. Under there." He reached for his glass and Jacques handed it to him and waited until he'd taken a drink.

"One last question, Rob." Jacques pulled out of his pocket the evidence bag containing the remains of the rakhi and placed it on the covers. "Do you recognise this?"

"It's mine," he said picking it up. "I hoped someone would find it and then find me."

Jacques smiled. "Beth Samuels found it."

Rob smiled. "The photographer. I remember. She was nice. I really liked her," he said and then let his head drop back on the pillow again. "I'm a bit tired."

"We can leave you now," said Pelletier. "And thank you. We will need to take a formal statement from you when you are feeling better. So I must ask you not to leave the area without letting us know."

"I don't think I'm going anywhere anytime soon," said Rob, the beginnings of a grin on his face.

As they walked down the corridor Pelletier pulled out his phone and ordered a search of the garden. Half way down the stairs, Jacques' phone rang and he picked up the call.

Jacques held onto Beth. "I thought I'd lost you." He stroked her long hair. "I really thought I'd lost you." He placed his finger under her chin and gently lifted her face so he could kiss her. Then he held her even tighter.

"I'd like to go, Jacques, if that's OK?"

He could hear the rasp in her normally soft voice. "Just one more minute," he said as he planted another kiss on the top of her head. "I'm not going to let go of you again." Then he took her hand in his and led her out of the hospital and to a waiting taxi.

"I presume the doctor told you that you had ingested a substance called atropine. I think the intention was to silence you because you found Rob's rakhi." He helped her into the back of the vehicle and sat beside her, clutching her hand in his and pressing it against his chest. "It was lucky that Fabian was at the Rouselles. He got to you just in time and the ambulance arrived eighteen minutes later and brought you to Mende." He looked at her and then kissed the back of her hand.

"It's OK. You can let go of my hand now." She smiled at him and as he put his arm around her shoulder she nestled up against him and rested her head on his chest.

Jacques had left Beth asleep on the settee in the loft. On the floor beside her, he'd set a tray containing a jug of water and a glass and some soft fruit on a plate. He strode through the village to Ferme Sithrez.

"Junior Gendarme Mancelle reporting for duty, sir," shouted Pierre as he cycled past Jacques and stopped just ahead of him.

Jacques saluted and smiled as Pierre got off his bike and tried to match Jacques' pace as he continued along the path to the top road.

Pelletier met him outside the farmhouse. "Beth all right?"

Jacques nodded. "She's at home resting." Remembering that Pierre was at his side, he squatted down to talk to him. "This is a real crime scene, Pierre, and I'm needed to help with the removal of evidence. So I—"

"Are there any dead bodies?" Pierre asked with an inappropriate enthusiasm whilst straining to see what might be going on inside.

Jacques suppressed a smirk and glanced up at Pelletier who was grinning.

"We don't know yet," he lied. "But the thing is, Pierre, only senior gendarmes are allowed at a crime scene so that means that I've no one to look after and patrol the village. So I need you to do that for me. OK?" He rose.

"Yes, sir," said Pierre and set off along the top road to ride around the village.

"You're really good with that boy, you know," said Pelletier. "Going to be a grand-father for the first time next month. It makes me feel old, Jacques."

They both walked back into the house and out the back

door and into the garden.

"What have we got so far?"

"Two bodies," said Clergue. "One male, one female, no visible signs of cause of death, but according to the pathologist this place is a witch's dream. There are all kinds of poisons and drugs that can be extracted from these plants, even with very basic equipment. We've just started on the second flower-bed at the top."

Pelletier took off his spectacles and used his crumpled handkerchief to clean the lenses. "Keep looking," he said to Clergue. "Jacques, I want you to go through the evidence we've found in the house. And if you think you can do that at Beth's that's fine by me. But confidentiality must be maintained."

"Thanks," said Jacques. He collected all the evidence bags together and took the steep track down to the gendarmerie. He changed out of his uniform and into jeans and a shirt, collected his laptop and went to Beth's chalet.

Creeping halfway up the stairs he could see that she was still asleep. He set up his office on the dining table.

He put the mobile phones back together and switched them on; only one had a flat battery. He decided he would deal with that later. The others, he could deduce from the contact lists and information he had on file belonged to Rob Myers, the two Swedes, but the last one had only one name and number in the contacts list, Gilles Fournier's.

"What a surprise," said Jacques as he stared at the display.

The file of papers was something else and, having sorted through everything and laid the items out on the table, he started to put them in chronological order. The couple of pages that were undated he put together to one side. The earliest piece was a cutting from a newspaper that contained a photograph of two children and a headline that read,

Terrible tragedy of child's death in frozen loch.

He looked at the two smiling faces staring out of the page

at him and there was something about the eyes of one of them that echoed with him. He was just about to read the article when he heard a light footfall above. "Beth, are you alright?"

"I'm fine," she said as she padded down the spiral stairs and came towards him. "What's all this?" She picked up a couple of items from the table as she walked round it.

"It's a file of papers I found at the Sithrez. I need to assimilate what we've got here." He pulled out the chair next to his for her to sit down.

"I'm feeling a bit wiped-out. And a bit useless. All this being looked-after isn't good for me." She looked at him accusingly.

"I'd better put you to work then."

thursday

Pelletier's office was crowded and stuffy with three people in it. He pushed the window wide open and then stood in front of it effectively blocking from Jacques and Clergue what little breeze there was.

"The initial report from the pathologist is that all the victims were poisoned, but the actual substance used in each case is yet to be determined," said Clergue.

"Do we know when we will have this?" asked Pelletier.

"Later today or tomorrow. And we have positive identification on all of the bodies," continued Clergue. "The oldest is Dieter Kellermann, the other two males are Anderson and Lavoie and the female is Ekstrom."

"Good," said Pelletier. "Jacques, what have you got?"

"I think we have a correct identification for the Sithrez, but their names have changed several times, it appears, and I still need to make some connections and check my assumptions. But I believe that Madame Sithrez was born Anastazja Kaminski." He presented the Magistrate with a copy of a newspaper article with key words and phrases highlighted for his attention. "The article states that Gosia Kaminski fell into a frozen loch in January 1957 whilst playing with her older sister Ana. It was the older child who alerted the parents to the tragedy and the coroner recorded a death by misadventure."

"Ah." Pelletier cleaned his glasses. "Go on."

"The next item is also a newspaper report. This time it concerns two deaths in a small terraced house in Newcastle. A woman beaten to death and a man garrotted with a cheese wire." Again he handed an annotated copy to the Magistrate. "The man and woman were husband and wife,

208

and there was a daughter. But the name at this point had become Canes. If you compare the photo of the two children in the first article with the picture in the second you will see it is an older Ana Kaminski. The report also states that the case is open and that no suspects have been identified. I've checked with Northumberland Police and the case is still open but only into the death of the father. Evidence gathered at the time suggested that he was probably responsible for the beating that caused his wife's death. Neighbours reported that he was often drunk and that she had been heard shouting and screaming earlier on the evening that she died."

"Ah. What happened to the child?"

"She was admitted to a children's home and there's a psychologist's report that shows that she had behavioural problems and that she was labelled as a sociopath. According to the Brits, the place was closed some years later and a major investigation followed which exposed widespread abuse amongst the supposed carers. The place was also renowned for its runaways. This next item is a copy of a coroner's report and I cannot understand how Madame Sithrez could have access to such an item. This relates to the death of Annie Matherson, a child who was killed by a hit and run driver. I'm checking with the British police to see if this case is closed or not."

"There are various other name changes but the most interesting is this last one to Ellen Matherson and the newspaper report into the death of a Mrs Mary Matherson. The report has stated that Mr and Mrs Matherson were present at the inquest and that Mrs Mary Matherson died as a result of tripping on the stairs at home and falling to her death. The lady was in her eighties and quite frail, it appears." He handed a copy of the report to Pelletier and drew his attention to the photograph. "That's Jean-Arnaud Sithrez, previously John Matherson. And if you look closely at the woman you will see there are clear resemblances between her and Madame Sithrez and the photos of Ana Kaminski."

"We need to interview Sithrez again, assuming he's mentally fit," said Pelletier.

"Yes, he is," said Clergue. "Confirmation came through just before this meeting."

"There's more," said Jacques. "Beth knows how to find details of marriages and deaths in England and she ran a search on the Internet for me. In the indices, there is a record of a marriage between Ellen Canning and a John Matherson in Newcastle some eighteen months before the date of that last newspaper article. We would need to see the registers themselves to get the precise date."

"Ah." The Magistrate returned to his desk and sat down. "So you seem to be suggesting that Madame Sithrez was involved in a number of serious accidental deaths. What are you thinking?"

"Exactly. Until we get the details surrounding each of those deaths, I can't be sure of what to think. But I do find it peculiar that the same person can be involved with or close to so many deaths. I've asked for information from the Brits for all of those names and cases. And why keep newspaper reports about such cases? If you felt guilty about the accident surely you would not want to have a constant reminder. But if the opposite were true...I don't know. These items could be some sort of trophy or record of triumph. But I'll just deal with the facts and let the psychologists puzzle that one out."

"Good work. Anything else?"

"The last item in the file I found at Ferme Sithrez is some sort of statement or diary. A lot of it is incoherent and there are names repeated over and over. But some of those names relate to the items I have just shown you. However, none of the names relate to the disappearances in the Vercors or Ariège."

"We'll interview Sithrez or Matherson this afternoon, Jacques" he said. "Thibault, get on with the rest of the paperwork and feed us anything that comes up as it arises.

"Do you recognise this?" Jacques placed on the table the

folder he had found at Ferme Sithrez.

"You know everything, then," was John's only response.

Pelletier shifted in his seat. "Yes, I think perhaps we do, Monsieur, but we still need you to clarify things for us." He folded his arms and fixed him with a stare.

"Can you confirm your name for us?" Jacques asked.

"John, John Matherson," he said. "She did everything. I only stopped her. That was all I did."

"Who did everything?"

"My wife, Ellen Matherson." John looked down at the table and shook his head. "I didn't know at first. I swear I didn't know at first." He covered his face with his hands. Jacques and Pelletier waited but John remained silent for a while. "But then there was Mum. I've always wondered about Mum."

"In what respect, John?"

"She had such difficulty getting up and down the stairs on her own. But Ellen was at home with her that day. She said she'd just gone out to the shops and was no more than half an hour. But when she got back there was Mum at the foot of the stairs, unconscious." He stopped and stared at the floor. "And then there were other things... The silences. I hated the silences. She would torture me with those silences for days on end. She'd ring up work and tell them I was ill and then lock all the doors. And then the..." He rolled up his shirtsleeves. The undersides of both his arms were covered in scars. "It just went on and on. But I couldn't let her hurt Beth, she reminded me so much of my little Annie."

"What happened to Annie?"

"Killed by a reckless driver. That's how I met Ellen. She worked at the Coroner's office then."

Jacques frowned and Pelletier took up the questioning.

"We've looked through the notebook and the names in there all relate to our missing persons files, John. But it doesn't help us to understand why."

John nodded. "She had to be in control. Always. It was a kind of war for her. Ridding herself of people she disliked.

People who wouldn't bend to her will. And it was because she knew she could."

friday

"How are you today?" Jacques came out from behind the counter as Beth walked in. He pulled her towards him and kissed her.

"I'm much better, and I want to talk to you," she said and stood back a little to release herself from his arms. "I've decided to go home tomorrow. I've checked with the ferry company and I can get a sailing on Sunday."

She saw his bright smile of a moment ago fade and disappear. He leant back against the counter and put his hands in his pockets.

"I also wanted to tell you that I've asked the estate agent to take the chalet off the market. You were right when you said that I could make the place my own. I've realised that it is my decision to sell or not." She went across to him and put her arms around him. "I will be back," she said. "In a couple of months or so. And I will keep in touch. Properly, this time."

it continues

I died beneath a clear autumn sky late in September 2007. Only midnight clouds cried for me as they brought the first sprinkling of snow to the tiny village of Messandrierre. I lie here, waiting.

Others have been found, but I'm still waiting. My name is Juan De Silva.

july 2009

Fantastic Books
Great Authors

darkstroke is
an imprint of
Crooked Cat Books

- Gripping Thrillers
- Cosy Mysteries
- Romantic Chick-Lit
- Fascinating Historicals
- Exciting Fantasy
- Young Adult and Children's
  Adventures
- Non-Fiction

Discover us online
www.darkstroke.com

Find us on instagram:
www.instagram.com/darkstrokebooks

Printed in Great Britain
by Amazon

29100149R00128